FOUND

THE MISSING: BOOK 1
FOUND

MARGARET PETERSON
HADDIX

SIMON & SCHUSTER BOOKS FOR YOUNG READERS

NEW YORK   LONDON   TORONTO   SYDNEY

SIMON & SCHUSTER BOOKS FOR YOUNG READERS
An imprint of Simon & Schuster Children's Publishing Division
1230 Avenue of the Americas, New York, New York 10020

Book design by Drew Willis
The text for this book is set in Weiss.
Manufactured in the United States of America
2 4 6 8 10 9 7 5 3 1
Library of Congress Cataloging-in-Publication Data
Haddix, Margaret Peterson.
Found / Margaret Peterson Haddix. — 1st ed.
p. cm. — (The missing ; [bk. 1])
Summary: When thirteen-year-old friends Jonah and Chip, who are both
adopted, find out that they were discovered on a plane that appeared out
of nowhere, full of babies, with no adults on board, they realize that
they have uncovered a mystery involving time travel and two opposing
forces, each trying to capture them.
ISBN-13: 978-1-4169-5417-0
ISBN-10: 1-4169-5417-1
[1. Adoption—Fiction. 2. Time travel—Fiction. 3. Science fiction.]
I. Title.
PZ7.H1164Fo 2008
[Fic]—dc22
2007023614

For my brothers

ACKNOWLEDGMENTS

With thanks to Steve Tuttle, vice president of communications for TASER International; and my friend Erin MacLellan, for answering my research questions. Thanks also to Nancy Roe Pimm, Jenny Patton, and Linda Stanek for their comments; and to my editor, David Gale; and agents, Tracey and Josh Adams, for having faith in my ideas before I did. And, finally, thanks to my family, for their many (mostly hilarious) plot suggestions. I am particularly grateful to my daughter, Meredith, for suggesting the plot twist that made everything work.

PROLOGUE

It wasn't there. Then it was.

Later, that was how Angela DuPre would describe the airplane—over and over, to one investigator after another—until she was told never to speak of it again.

But when she first saw the plane that night, she wasn't thinking about mysteries or secrets. She was wondering how many mistakes she could make without getting fired, how many questions she dared ask before her supervisor, Monique, would explode, "That's it! You're too stupid to work at Sky Trails Air! Get out of here!" Angela had used a Post-it note to write down the code for standby passengers who'd received a seat assignment at the last minute, and she'd stuck it to her computer screen. She knew she had. But somehow, between the flight arriving from Saint Louis and the one leaving for Chicago, the Post-it had vanished. Any minute now, she thought, some standby passenger would show up at the counter asking for a boarding pass, and Angela would be forced to turn to Monique once more and mumble, "Uh, what was that code again?" And then Monique, who had perfect hair and perfect nails and a perfect tan and had probably been born knowing all the Sky Trails codes, would grit her teeth and narrow her eyes and repeat the code in that slow fake-patient voice she'd been using with Angela all night, the voice that said behind the words, *I know you're severely mentally challenged, so I will try not to speak faster than one word per minute, but you have to realize, this is a real strain for me because I am so vastly superior. . . .*

Angela was not severely mentally challenged. She'd done fine in school and at the Sky Trails orientation. It was just, this was her first actual day on the job, and Monique had been nasty from the very start. Every one of Monique's frowns and glares and insinuations kept making Angela feel more panicky and stupid.

Sighing, Angela glanced up. She needed a break from staring at the computer screen longing for a lost Post-it. She peered out at the passengers crowding the terminal: tired-looking families sprawled in seats, dark-suited businessmen sprinting down the aisle. Which one of them would be the standby flier who'd rush up to the counter and ruin Angela's life? Generally speaking, Angela had always liked people; she wasn't used to seeing them as threats. She forced her gaze beyond the clumps of passengers, to the huge plate glass window on the other side of the aisle. It was getting dark out, and Angela could see the runway lights twinkling in the distance.

Runway, runaway, she thought vaguely. And then—had she blinked?—suddenly the lights were gone. No, she corrected herself, *blocked.* Suddenly there was an airplane between Angela and the runway lights, an airplane rolling rapidly toward the terminal.

Angela gasped.

"What now?" Monique snarled, her voice thick with exasperation.

"That plane," Angela said. "At gate 2B. I thought it—" What was she supposed to say? *Wasn't there? Appeared out of thin air?*"—I thought it was going too fast and might run into the building," she finished in a rush, because suddenly that had seemed true too. She watched as the plane pulled to a stop, neatly aligned with the jetway. "But it . . . didn't. No worries."

Monique whirled on Angela.

"Never," she began, in a hushed voice full of suppressed rage, "never, ever, ever say anything like that. Weren't you paying attention in orientation? Never say you think a plane is going to crash. Never say a plane could crash. Never even use the word *crash*. Do you understand?"

"Okay," Angela whispered. "Sorry."

But some small rebellious part of her brain was thinking, *I didn't use the word* crash. *Weren't you paying attention to me? And if a plane really was going to run into the building, wouldn't Sky Trails want its employees to warn people, to get them out of the way?*

Just as rebelliously, Angela kept watching the plane parked at 2B, instead of bending her head back down to concentrate on her computer.

"Um, Monique?" she said after a few moments. "Should one of us go over there and help the passengers unload—er, I mean—deplane?" She was proud of herself for remembering to use the official airline-sanctioned word for unloading.

Beside her, Monique rolled her eyes.

"The gate agents responsible for 2B," she said in a tight voice, "will handle deplaning there."

Angela glanced at the 2B counter, which was silent and dark and completely unattended. There wasn't even a message scrolling across the LCD sign behind the counter to indicate that the plane had arrived or where it'd come from.

"Nobody's there," Angela said stubbornly.

Frowning, Monique finally glanced up.

"Great. Just great," she muttered. "I always have to fix everyone else's mistakes." She began stabbing her perfectly manicured nails at her computer keyboard. Then she stopped, mid-stab. "Wait—that can't be right."

"What is it?" Angela asked.

Monique was shaking her head.

"Must be pilot error," she said, grimacing in disgust. "Some yahoo pulled up to the wrong gate. There's not supposed to be anyone at that gate until the Cleveland flight at nine thirty."

Angela considered telling Monique that if Sky Trails had banned *crash* from their employees' vocabulary, that maybe passengers should be protected from hearing *pilot error* as well. But Monique was already grabbing the telephone, barking out orders.

"Yeah, Bob, major screwup," she was saying. "You've got to get someone over here. . . . No, I don't know which gate it was supposed to go to. How would I know? Do you think I'm clairvoyant? . . . No, I can't see the numbers on the plane. Don't you know it's dark out?"

With her free hand, Monique was gesturing frantically at Angela.

"At least go open the door!" she hissed.

"You mean . . ."

"The door to the jetway!" Monique said, pointing. Angela hoped that some of the contempt on Monique's face was intended for Bob, not just her. Angela imagined meeting Bob someday, sharing a laugh at Monique's expense. Still, dutifully, she walked over to the 2B waiting area and pulled open the door to the hallway that led down to the plane.

Nobody came out.

Angela picked a piece of lint off her blue skirt and then stood at attention, her back perfectly straight, just like in the training videos. Maybe she couldn't keep track of standby codes, but she was capable of standing up straight.

Still, nobody appeared.

Angela began to feel foolish, standing so alertly by an open door that no one was using. She bent her head and peeked down the jetway—it was deserted and turned at such an angle that she couldn't see all the way down to the plane, to see if anyone had opened the door to the jet yet. She backed up a little and peered out the window, straight down to the cockpit of the plane. The cockpit was dark, its windows blank, and that struck Angela as odd. She'd been on the job for only five hours, and she'd been a little distracted. But she was pretty sure that when planes landed, the pilots stayed in the cockpit for a while filling out paperwork or something. She thought that they at least waited until all the passengers were off before they turned out the cockpit lights.

Angela peeked down the empty jetway once more and went back to Monique.

"Of course I'm sure there's a plane at that gate! I can see it with my own eyes!" Monique was practically screaming into the phone. She shook her head at Angela, and for the first time it was almost in a companionable way, as if to say, *At least you know there's a plane there! Unlike the other morons I have to deal with!* Monique cupped her hand over the receiver and fumed to Angela, "The incompetence around here is unbelievable! The control tower says that plane never landed, never showed up on the radar. The Sky Trails dispatcher says we're not missing a plane—everything that was supposed to land in the past hour pulled up to the right gate, and all the other planes due to arrive within the next hour or so are accounted for. How could so many people just lose a plane?"

Or, how could we find it? Angela thought. The whole situation was beginning to seem strange to her, otherworldly. But maybe that was just a function of being new to the job, of having spent so much time concentrating on the computer and being yelled at by Monique. Maybe airports lost and found planes all the time, and that was just one of those things nobody had mentioned in the Sky Trails orientation.

"Did, uh, anybody try to contact the pilot?" Angela asked cautiously.

"Of course!" Monique said. "But there's no answer. He must be on the wrong frequency."

Angela thought of the dark cockpit, the way she hadn't been able to see through the windows. She decided not to mention this.

"Should I go back and wait? . . ."

Monique nodded fiercely and went back to yelling into the phone: "What do you mean, this isn't your responsibility? It's not my responsibility either!"

Angela was glad to put a wide aisle and two waiting areas between herself and Monique again. She went back to the jetway door by gate 2B. The sloped hallway leading down to the plane was still empty, and the colorful travel posters lining the walls—"Sky Trails! Your ticket to the world!"—seemed jarringly bright. Angela stepped into the jetway.

I'll just go down far enough to see if the jet door is open, she told herself. *It may be a violation of protocol, but Monique won't notice, not when she's busy yelling at everyone else in the airport. . . .*

At the bend in the ramp, Angela looked around the corner. She had a limited view, but caught a quick glimpse of a flight attendants' little galley, with neatly stowed drink carts. Obviously, the jet door was standing wide open. She started to turn around, already beginning to debate with herself about whether she should report this information to Monique. Then she heard—what? A whimper? A cry?

Angela couldn't exactly identify the sound, but it was enough to pull her on down the jetway.

New Sky Trails employee saves passenger on first day on job, she thought to herself, imagining the praise and congratulations—and maybe the raise—she'd be sure to receive if what she was visualizing was real. She'd learned CPR in the orientation session. She knew basic first aid. She knew where every emergency phone in the airport was located. She started walking faster, then running.

On the side of the jet, she was surprised to see a strange insignia: TACHYON TRAVEL, it said, some airline Angela had never heard of. Was that a private charter company maybe? And then, while she was staring at it, the words suddenly changed into the familiar wing-in-the-clouds symbol of Sky Trails.

Angela blinked.

That couldn't have happened, she told herself. *It was just an optical illusion, just because I was running, just because I'm worried about whoever made that cry or whimper. . . .*

Angela stepped onto the plane. She turned her head

first to the left, looking into the cockpit. Its door also stood open, but the small space was empty, the instruments dark.

"Hello?" Angela called, looking to the right now, expecting to see some flight attendant with perfectly applied makeup—or maybe some flight attendant and a pilot bent over a prone passenger, maybe an old man suddenly struck down by a heart attack or a stroke. Or, at the very least, passengers crowding the aisle, clutching laptops and stuffed animals brought from faraway grandparents' homes, overtired toddlers crying, fragile old women calling out to taller men, "Could you pull my luggage down from the overhead for me? It's that red suitcase over there. . . ."

But the aisle of this airplane was as empty and silent as its cockpit. Angela could see all the way to the back of the plane, and not a single person stood in her view, not a single voice answered her.

Only then did Angela drop her gaze to the passenger seats. They stretched back twelve rows, with two seats per row on the left side of the aisle and one each on the right. She stepped forward, peering at all of them. Thirty-six seats on this plane, and every single one of them was full.

Each seat contained a baby.

THIRTEEN YEARS LATER

ONE

"You don't look much like your sister," Chip said, bouncing the basketball low against the driveway.

Jonah waited to answer until he'd darted his hand in and stolen the basketball away.

"Adopted," he said, shooting the ball toward the backboard. But the angle was wrong, and the ball bounced off the hoop.

"Really? You or her? Or both?" Chip asked, snagging the rebound.

"Me," Jonah said. "Just me." Then he sneaked a glance at Chip, to see if this made a difference. It didn't to Jonah—he'd always known he was adopted, and as far as he was concerned, it wasn't much more of a deal than his liking mint chocolate-chip ice cream while Katherine liked orange sherbet. But sometimes other people got weird about it.

Chip had one eyebrow raised, like he was still processing the information. This gave Jonah a chance to grab the ball again.

"Hey, if you're not, like, related by blood or anything, does that mean you could date her?" Chip asked.

Jonah almost dropped the ball.

"Yuck—*no!*" he said. "That's sick!"

"Why?" Chip asked.

"Because she's my sister! Ugh!" If Chip had asked him that question a few years ago, Jonah would have added, "And she's got cooties!" But Jonah was in seventh grade now, and seventh graders didn't talk about cooties. Anyhow Jonah hadn't known Chip a few years ago—Chip had moved into the neighborhood just three months ago, in the summertime. It was kind of a new thing for Chip to come over and play basketball.

Carefully, Jonah began bouncing the ball again.

"If you think me and Katherine don't look alike, you should see my cousin Mia," he said.

"Why?" Chip asked. "Is she even cuter than Katherine?"

Jonah made a face.

"She's only four years old!" he said. "And she's Chinese. My aunt and uncle had to go to Beijing to adopt her."

He could remember, the whole time Aunt Joan and Uncle Brad were arranging to adopt Mia—filling out the paperwork, sending away for the visas, crossing dates off calendars, and then buying new calendars to cross off new dates—his own mom and dad had spent a lot of time hugging him and exclaiming, "We were so lucky, getting you! Such a miracle!"

Katherine had been jealous.

Jonah could just picture her standing in the kitchen at age five or six, wispy blond pigtails sticking out on both sides of her head, a scowl on her face, complaining, "Weren't you lucky to get me, too? Aren't *I* a miracle?"

Mom had bent down and kissed her.

"Of course you're a miracle too," she said. "A big miracle. But we had nine months to know you were coming. With Jonah, we thought it would be years and years and years before we'd get a baby, and then that call came out of the blue—"

"The week before Christmas—" Dad added.

"And they said we could have him right away, and he was so cute, with his big eyes and his dimples and all that brown hair—"

"And then a year later, lovely Katherine came along—" Dad reached over and put his arm around her waist, pulling her close, until she giggled. "And we had a boy and a girl, and we were so happy because we had everything we wanted."

Jonah's parents could be so sappy. He didn't have too many gripes about them—as parents went, they were pretty decent. But they told that story way too often about how excited they'd been, getting that call out of the blue, getting Jonah.

Also, if he was listing grievances, he often wished that they'd had the sense *not* to name him after a guy who got swallowed up by a whale. But that was kind of a minor thing.

Now he aimed carefully and sent the ball whooshing through the net. It went through cleanly—the perfect shot.

Chip flopped down onto the grass beside the driveway.

"Man," he said. "You're going to make the basketball team for sure."

Jonah caught the ball as it fell through the net.

"Who says I'm trying out?"

Chip leaned forward.

"Well, aren't you?" he asked. "You've got to! That's, like, what everyone wants! The basketball players get all the chicks!"

This sounded so ridiculous coming out of Chip's mouth that Jonah fell into the grass laughing. After a moment, Chip started laughing too. It was like being a little kid again, rolling around in the grass laughing, not caring at all about who might see you.

Jonah stopped laughing and sat up. He peered up and down the street—fortunately, nobody was around to see them. He whacked Chip on the arm.

"So," he said. "Do you have a crush on my sister?"

Chip shrugged, which might mean, "Yes," or "Would I tell you if I did?" or "I haven't decided yet." Jonah wasn't sure he wanted to know anyway. He and Chip weren't really good friends yet, but Chip having a crush on Katherine could make everything very weird.

Chip lay back in the grass, staring up at the back of the basketball hoop.

"Do you ever wonder what's going to happen?" he asked. "I mean, I really, really want to make the basketball team. But even if I make it in seventh and eighth grades, then there's high school to deal with. Whoa. And then there's college, and being a grown-up. . . . It's all pretty scary, don't you think?"

"You forgot about planning your funeral," Jonah said.

"What?"

"You know. If you're going to get all worried about being a grown-up, you might as well figure out what's going to happen when you're ninety years old and you die," Jonah said. Personally, Jonah didn't like to plan anything.

Sometimes, at the breakfast table, his mom would ask the whole family what they wanted for dinner. Even that was way too much planning for Jonah.

Chip opened his mouth to answer, then shut it abruptly and stared hard at the front door of Jonah's house. The door was opening slowly. Then Katherine stuck her head out.

"Hey, Jo-No," she called, using the nickname she knew would annoy him. "Mom says to get the mail."

Jonah tried to remember if he'd seen the mail truck gliding through the neighborhood. Maybe when he and Chip were concentrating on shooting hoops? He hoped it wasn't when they were rolling around in the grass laughing and making fools of themselves. But he obediently jumped up and went over to the mailbox, pulling out a small stack of letters and ads. He carried the mail up to Katherine.

"You can take it on in to Mom, can't you?" he asked mockingly. "Or is that too much work for Princess Katherine?"

After what he and Chip had been talking about, it was a little hard to look her in the eye. When he thought about the name Katherine, he still pictured her as she'd been a few years ago, with pudgy cheeks and those goofy-looking pigtails. Now that she was in sixth grade, she'd . . . changed. She'd slimmed down and shot up and started worrying about clothes. Her hair had gotten thicker and turned more of a golden color, and she spent a lot of time in her room with the door shut, straightening her hair or curling it or something. Right now she was even wearing makeup: a tiny smear of brown over her eyes, black on her eyelashes, a smudge of red on her cheeks.

Weird, weird, weird.

"Hey, Jo-no-brain, can't you read?" Katherine asked, as annoying as ever. "This one's for you."

She pulled a white envelope off the top of the stack of mail and shoved it back into his hands. It did indeed say *Jonah Skidmore* on the address label, but it wasn't the type of mail he usually got. Usually if he got mail, it was just postcards or brochures, reminding him about school events or basketball leagues or Boy Scout camp-outs. This envelope looked very formal and official, like an important notice.

"Who's it from?" Katherine asked.

"It doesn't say." That was strange too. He flipped the envelope over and ripped open the flap. He pulled out one thin sheet of paper.

"Let me see," Katherine said, jostling against him and knocking the letter out of his hand.

The letter fluttered slowly down toward the threshold

of the door, but Jonah had already read every single word on the page.

There were only six:

YOU ARE ONE OF THE MISSING.

TWO

Katherine snorted.

"Missing link, maybe," she said.

Jonah reached down and picked up the letter. By the time he'd straightened up again, Chip had joined him on the porch, either because he was curious about the letter too, or because he really did have a crush on Katherine.

"What's that?" Chip asked.

Jonah shrugged.

"Just a prank, I guess," he said. Seventh grade was all about pranks. You could always tell when someone in the neighborhood was having a sleepover, because then the kids who weren't invited suddenly had gobs of toilet paper in all the trees in their yards. Or their cell phones rang at midnight: "I'm watching you. . . ." followed by gales of laughter.

"Pranks are supposed to be funny," Katherine objected. "What's funny about that?"

"Nothing," Chip said. Jonah noticed that Chip was smiling at Katherine, not looking at the letter.

"Now, maybe if it said, 'It's ten o'clock—do you know where your brain is?' or 'Missing: one brain cell. Please return to Jonah Skidmore. It's all I've got'—maybe *that* would be funny," Katherine said. She yanked the letter out of Jonah's hand. "Give me a few minutes. I could turn this into a really good prank."

Jonah snatched the letter back.

"That's okay," he said, and crammed the letter into his jeans pocket.

He knew it was just a prank—it had to be—but for just a second, staring at those words, *You are one of the missing,* he'd almost believed them. Especially since he'd just been telling Chip about being adopted. . . . What if somebody really *was* missing him? He didn't know anything about his birth parents; all the adoption records had been sealed. He'd had such trouble understanding that when he was a little kid. He'd been a little obsessed with animals back then, so first he'd pictured elephant seals waddling on top of official-looking papers. Then, when his parents explained it a little better, he pictured crates in locked rooms, the doors covered with Easter Seals.

He'd been a pretty strange little kid.

In fact—his face burned a little at the memory—he'd even given a report in second grade on all the different uses of the word *seal*, from Arctic ice seals to Navy Seals to sealed adoption records. The report had included the line, "And so, that's why it's interesting that I'm adopted, because it makes me unique." His parents had helped him with that one.

Wait a minute—Tony McGilicuddy had been in his second-grade class, and so had Jacob Hanes and Dustin Cravers. . . . What if they remembered too? What if they'd sent this letter because of that?

Jonah narrowed his eyes at Katherine, who took a step back under the intensity of his gaze.

"You know what?" he said, glaring at her. "You're right. This isn't funny at all." He pulled the letter back out of his pocket and ripped it into shreds. He dropped the shreds into Katherine's hand. "Throw that away for me, okay?"

"Um . . . okay," she said, apparently too surprised to think of a smart-alecky comeback.

"Want to come out and play basketball with us when you're done?" Chip asked, as she started to close the door.

Katherine tilted her head to the side, considering. Jonah figured she was adding up all the possibilities: *seventh* grader acting interested plus a chance to tick off older brother plus a chance to show off. (For a girl, Katherine was pretty good at basketball.) It seemed like a no-brainer to Jonah. But Katherine shook her head.

"No, thanks. I just did my nails," she said, and pulled the door all the way shut.

Chip groaned.

"She's your sister," he said. "Tell me—is she playing hard to get?"

"Who knows?" Jonah said, but he wasn't thinking about Katherine.

By dinnertime Jonah had convinced himself that Tony McGilicuddy and Jacob Hanes and Dustin Cravers were a bunch of idiots, and he didn't really care what they thought or did. They could send him stupid letters all they wanted; it didn't matter to him. He stabbed his fork into his mashed potatoes and savored the sound of the metal tines hitting the plate. He didn't pay much attention to what Mom and Dad and Katherine were talking about—something about some brand of jeans that all the popular girls in sixth grade owned.

"But, honey, you're popular, and you don't have those jeans, so you can't be right about all the popular girls having them," Mom argued.

"Mo-om," Katherine said.

Then the doorbell rang.

For a moment, everybody froze, Dad and Jonah with forkfuls of food halfway to their mouths, Mom and Katherine in mid-argument. The doorbell rang again, one urgent peal after another.

"I'll get it," Jonah said, standing up.

"Whoever it is, tell them to come back later. It's din-nertime," Mom said. Mom always made a big deal about family dinners. The way that certain other parents made their kids go to church, Jonah's parents made him and Katherine sit down at the dinner table with them just about every night. (*And* they usually had to go to church, too.)

Jonah realized he was still holding his fork, so he stuck it into his mouth as he walked to the door—no point in wasting perfectly good mashed potatoes. It didn't take him long to gulp them down, lick the fork one last time, and then transfer the fork to his other hand so he could grab the doorknob. But the doorbell rang three more times before he yanked the door back.

It was Chip standing on the porch. At first he didn't even seem to notice that the door was open, he was so focused on pounding his hand against the doorbell.

"Hey," Jonah said.

Finally Chip stopped hitting the doorbell. The chimes

kept ringing behind Jonah for a few extra seconds.

"I've got to talk to you," Chip said.

He was breathing hard, like he'd run all the way from his house, six driveways down the street. He shoved his hands through his curly blond hair—maybe trying to wipe away sweat, maybe trying to restore some order to the mess. It didn't help. The curls stuck out in all directions. And Chip kept darting his eyes around, like he couldn't keep them trained on any one thing for more than an instant.

"Okay," Jonah said. "We're eating right now, but later on—"

Chip clutched Jonah's T-shirt.

"I can't wait," he said. "You've got to help me. Please."

Jonah peeled Chip's fingers off the shirt.

"Um, sure," Jonah said. "Calm down. What do you want to talk about?"

Chip's darting eyes took in the houses on either side of Jonah's. He peered down the long hallway to the kitchen, where he could probably see just the edge of the dinner table.

"Not here," Chip said, lowering his voice. "We've got to talk *privately*. Somewhere no one will hear us."

Jonah glanced back over his shoulder. He could see the perfectly crisped fried chicken leg lying on his plate beside his half-eaten potatoes. He could also see Katherine, peering curiously around the corner at him.

"All right," Jonah said. "Wait here for just a second."

He went back to the table.

"Mom, Dad, may I be excused?" he asked.

"No clean plate club for you," Katherine taunted, which was really stupid. Mom and Dad had stopped making a big deal about clean plates years ago, after Mom read some article about childhood obesity.

"I'll put everything in the refrigerator and eat it later," Jonah said, picking up his plate.

"I'll take care of that," Mom said quietly, taking the plate and fork from him. "Go on and help Chip."

Jonah cast one last longing glance at the chicken and went back to the front door. He'd kind of wanted Mom and Dad to say no, he wasn't allowed to leave the table. He didn't know what anyone thought he could do to help Chip. The way Chip was acting, it was like he was going to confess a murder. Or maybe it was something like, he just found out that his parents were splitting up and he had to decide which one to live with. Jonah knew a kid that had happened to. It was awful. But Jonah couldn't give advice about anything like that.

Chip practically had his face pressed against the glass of the front door, watching Jonah come back.

"Come on," Jonah said. "Let's go to my room."

This was strange too because Chip had never been in Jonah's room before. They were play-basketball-in-the-driveway-and-maybe-come-into-the-kitchen-for-a-drink-of-water friends, not let's-go-hang-out-in-my-room friends. Jonah held the front door open for Chip, and then Chip followed him up the stairs. Chip didn't even glance around when they got to Jonah's room. Which was good—maybe he wouldn't notice that along with his sports posters, Jonah still had one up from third grade that showed a LEGO roller coaster.

Jonah shut the door and sat down on the bed. Chip sank into the desk chair.

"I got one, too," Chip said. He was clutching his face now, almost like that kid in the *Home Alone* movie.

"One what?" Jonah asked.

"One of those letters. About being missing."

Chip pulled a piece of paper out of his pocket. Jonah could tell that Chip had already folded and unfolded it many times: the creases were beginning to fray. Chip unfolded it once more, and Jonah could see that it was just like the letter he'd gotten, six typewritten words on an otherwise blank sheet of paper:

YOU ARE ONE OF THE MISSING.

"Chip, it's a *prank*," Jonah said. "A joke that's not even funny." But he was thinking, *Chip wasn't in that second grade class with Dustin and Jacob and Tony. He's not adopted, I don't think. So this is really stupid.* Jonah leaned back against the wall, more relaxed than he'd been in hours. "It's *nothing*," he told Chip.

"Yeah, that's what I thought," Chip said. "You know what the worst thing is? I was even kind of happy when I pulled this out of the mailbox. Like, 'Hey, I'm not just the new kid anymore. Somebody's actually noticed me enough to try to play a prank on me. A stupid prank, but still.'"

Jonah shrugged.

"So, stay happy," he said. "Congratulations. You got a prank letter."

Chip bolted forward, his face suddenly hard.

"No," he said. "No. 'Cause, see, then I went inside. And my dad was standing there, and I was like, 'Look, Dad, I got this prank letter.' And then I'm telling him all about it, about how you got the same letter, and you'd just told me about being adopted, and I could tell you were kind of mad about this letter, and I thought it might be because you're sensitive about the whole adoption thing—"

"No, I'm not!" Jonah said.

Chip ignored him.

"And you ripped up the letter and threw the pieces in your sister's face—"

"I did not! Not in her *face!*"

Chip kept talking, as if Jonah hadn't said a word.

"And I'm just going on and on, about how obviously the letter had nothing to do with you being adopted because *I* got the same letter and *I'm* not adopted and—and— I don't know what I was thinking, because then I said, 'Right, Dad? I'm not adopted, am I, Dad?' And then my dad said . . . my dad said . . ."

Chip's mouth kept moving, but no sound came out. It was like he'd run out of words. Or at least run out of words he wanted to say.

Jonah froze, sitting very precisely in the center of his bed.

"What did your dad say?" he asked very carefully.

Chip was staring straight ahead, his eyes vacant.

"*Are* you adopted?" Jonah whispered.

Wordlessly, Chip nodded.

THREE

"Well, why didn't you tell me that this afternoon?" Jonah asked. He felt kind of silly. It was like when he was on the swim team and some of his friends had hidden his clothes, so he had to walk through the rec center lobby wearing nothing but a Speedo while everyone else was fully clothed. "I told you I was adopted—why didn't you tell me?"

"I didn't know!" Chip exploded. His whole face was red. "Mom and Dad never told me anything! All this time I thought my parents were my real parents—"

"They're still your real parents," Jonah corrected automatically.

"They are not!" Chip said furiously. "They're total strangers to me now! How could they not tell me?"

That wasn't a question Jonah could answer. After a

certain point, he'd stopped reading all the kid-approved "Isn't adoption wonderful!" books his parents had bought for him and had started sneaking peeks at some of the books on their bookshelves: *Raising the Well-Adjusted Adopted Child, What to Tell Your Adopted and Foster Children, Adoption Without Secrets*. All the adoptive-parents books Jonah had ever seen acted like there was one commandment Moses had forgotten to bring down from Mount Sinai: tell adopted kids the truth.

Chip was running his hands violently through his hair again. If he kept that up, he'd end up pulling it all out.

"Stop that," Jonah said. "Your parents probably thought they were doing the right thing."

Chip laughed bitterly.

"Yeah—the right thing for *them*." He stood up abruptly, knocking the desk chair over backward. "This is just like them. They always want to pretend that everything's *normal*, that everything's *fine*: 'No, Chip, you didn't hear anyone yelling last night. Your father and I never fight—'"

"Adoption is normal," Jonah said stiffly. "It's been part of human society for centuries."

Chip shot him a "get real" look and began pacing. When he reached Jonah's door, he pounded his fists on the wood. Then he lowered his forehead onto his fists and just stood there.

"Uh, Chip?" Jonah said nervously. "Are you okay?"

"You know what's funny?" Chip said in a strangled voice, without lifting his head. "It's kind of a relief . . . not being related to them. I don't want to be like Mom and Dad, anyhow. But who am I for real? Who are my real parents?"

"Birth parents," Jonah said quietly. "They're called birth parents."

Chip rolled his head to the side.

"Would you stop that?" he said. "It's like you're brainwashed or something."

"What?" Jonah said defensively. "Those are the correct terms. Birth parents are the people who give birth to you. Real parents are the ones who change your diapers and get up in the middle of the night when you're a baby and show you how to ride a bike without training wheels and, and. . . ." He stopped because he thought maybe he was quoting directly from *What to Tell Your Adopted and Foster Children*.

Chip slid down to the floor, crumpling like one of those rag dolls Katherine used to drag around by the feet.

"My parents didn't show me how to ride a bike," he said. "They left that to the babysitter."

Jonah thought for a moment.

"Well, at least they were the ones who paid the babysitter."

Chip groaned. He balled his hands into fists again and pressed them against his eye sockets.

"Why?" he whispered. "Why did my real parents give me up?"

This time, Jonah didn't bother correcting Chip out loud, though his brain translated, *You mean, your birth mother set up an adoption plan. . . .*

"You know, there are lots of reasons people can't take care of their own kids," Jonah said cautiously. "Maybe your birth parents died. Maybe you're adopted from Russia or someplace like that, where things are different." He waited a second. Chip didn't move. "Maybe . . . maybe now that you know you're adopted, your mom and dad might tell you more about your story, if they know it. Sometimes, even if the records are sealed at the time of the adoption, people change their minds and decide they want to be more open. . . ."

Okay, now Jonah was almost certain that he was quoting directly from one of his parents' books.

Chip began shaking his head again, so hard it rattled the door behind him. Then he glared over at Jonah, his eyes burning.

"My dad said—" Chip choked, swallowed hard, tried again, "—my dad said I didn't need to know anything else. He said he never wanted to talk about this again."

And then Jonah felt the anger boiling up inside of him. Jonah didn't get mad often. He'd never met Chip's dad, just seen him drive by. (He drove a nice car—a BMW.) Jonah probably couldn't have picked Chip's dad out in a line-up. But right now Jonah wanted to stalk over to Chip's house, swing his best punch, and hit Chip's dad right in the mouth. He wanted to hit him a couple of times.

Jonah clenched his fists. Chip was still staring up at him, but his expression had slipped over into helplessness now—helplessness and hopelessness.

"What can I do?" Chip asked.

"When you're a grown-up," Jonah said, "you can try to find your birth parents. You won't need your mom and dad's permission for anything then. And until then—until then, I swear, I'll do everything I can to help you."

FOUR

"Try 10-28-66," Chip whispered.

"Why?" Jonah asked.

"That's Dad's birthday," Chip said. "He's so conceited and stupid, he'd use his own birthday as the code."

It'd been two days since Jonah and Chip had each gotten their "YOU ARE ONE OF THE MISSING" letters, and Chip was acting crazier than ever. Today, coming home on the school bus, Chip had gotten obsessed with the idea that he had to see his birth certificate, that it would tell him everything he needed to know. So now the two boys were crouched beside a wall safe in Chip's basement.

Jonah paused with his fingers poised over the digital keypad.

"Really," he said, "even if your birth certificate's in

here, it's not going to help. Like I told you—like it said on the Internet—when a kid's adopted, they issue a new certificate and lock all the old papers away. Your original birth certificate's not going to be in here unless it was an open adoption and somehow, I don't think, if your parents won't even talk about you being adopted—"

"Just try the code," Chip insisted. "My hand's shaking too bad."

Jonah glanced over at his friend, who did indeed look shaky. Even in the dim light of the basement, Jonah could tell that Chip had a panicky sheen of sweat on his face. Chip's curly hair was mashed down because he kept clutching his head, like he had to work hard to hold himself together. He seemed about one step away from being one of those loony types who mumbled to themselves on the street downtown.

Jonah sighed and began punching in numbers: 1 0 2 8 6 6.

Nothing happened.

"When's your birthday?" Jonah asked.

"Mine?" Chip said. "September nineteenth."

"And you're thirteen?"

"Yeah, why?"

Jonah didn't answer, just began punching in a new combination: 0 9 1 9 . . .

The safe beeped, then there was audible click. The safe door sprang open, just a crack.

"Bingo!" Jonah said. He kind of wished his own mom or dad were there just then, because they would be able to tell Chip, "See? Your parents must care about you some, if they use your birthday as the code to their safe." But Jonah couldn't say anything that goopy himself.

"Go ahead and open it," Chip said. "I can't look."

He had his shaking hand over his eyes, but he kept lifting it to peek out.

Jonah gripped the door to the partly open safe.

"Are you sure you want me to do this?" he asked. "This is like breaking and entering or something."

Chip scowled at him.

"You're in *my* house," he said. "I *asked* you to open the safe."

"But your parents—"

"What they want doesn't count," Chip said harshly.

There was some saying Jonah's mom always quoted—usually to Katherine—about how eavesdroppers never heard anything good about themselves. Jonah wondered if that also applied to boys opening locked safes and looking at secret papers. But that was something else he couldn't say to Chip. He jerked on the door, swinging it completely open, and reached in to take out the first few sheets of paper on top of the stack.

"This is just stuff about buying your house," Jonah said, leafing quickly through the papers. "Real estate settlements, title insurance . . ."

Chip moved his hand away from his eyes and squinted at the papers.

"Maybe that's connected too," he said slowly. "My dad says they got a really sweet deal for this house. Maybe I was supposed to meet you, so that I'd find out about being adopted. . . ."

Jonah carefully put the house papers in a stack on the floor.

"About four out of every one hundred Americans are adopted," Jonah said. "I think you could have met someone who was adopted in *any* neighborhood you might have moved to. Now you're sounding really crazy, like those conspiracy theorists who think the moon landing never happened, or that the government has a bunch of aliens locked up on some military base in New Mexico."

"But they *do*," Chip said. "Those aliens are real."

"You really believe that?"

Chip slugged him in the arm.

"No. Fooled you!"

Jonah was glad that Chip could still show some sense of humor, that he hadn't totally crossed the line into insanity. Jonah reached into the safe again and pulled out more papers. He was careful to keep them in order as he sorted through them.

Three-fourths of the way down into the stack, he let out a low whistle.

"Here it is."

He held up a document labeled, BIRTH CERTIFICATE— Cook County, Illinois.

Chip evidently forgot that he was too stressed out to look. He crowded against Jonah's shoulder.

"Charles Haddingford Winston the third, huh?" Jonah teased.

Chip grimaced.

"Crazy, isn't it?" he said bitterly. "I'm Charles Winston the third, and I'm not even related. They just had to have some kid to stick that name on."

"Chip, you *are* related. Or, as good as related. They've *raised* you," Jonah said.

"Not very well," Chip said.

Jonah took one look at Chip's face and decided not to argue.

He rifled through the rest of the papers. Beside him, Chip groaned.

"'Happy Family Adoption Agency'?" Chip muttered. "You have got to be kidding."

Something slipped out of the stack of papers Jonah

was holding against one knee, while he braced his other knee against the floor. Trying to catch the one sliding paper, Jonah lost his balance and fell over sideways. The whole stack cascaded down to the carpet, skidding toward the wall.

"Sorry," Jonah said. "If things are out of order, your dad's going to be able to tell—"

"I don't care," Chip said acidly.

Jonah frowned and began gathering up the papers. He thought he'd gotten everything until he saw a scrap of yellow sticking out from under a chair a few feet away.

"That's what started this whole mess," he muttered. He reached under the chair and pulled out a yellow Post-it note. It said, *James Reardon, (513) 555-0192*. He held the note up so Chip could see it too.

"Was this with the adoption papers or the house stuff?" Jonah asked.

Chip narrowed his eyes.

"I know how to find out," he said.

He took the Post-it note from Jonah's hand and walked to the other side of the basement, where couches and chairs clustered around a huge entertainment center. He reached into a cabinet of the entertainment center and pulled out a cordless phone.

"Here—I'll put it on speakerphone so you can hear too," Chip said.

"Chip, I don't think—" Jonah stopped, because he couldn't explain why this suddenly seemed like such a bad idea to him.

Chip was already punching in numbers, each digital beep adding to Jonah's sense of apprehension. Jonah rushed over to Chip's side, as if being able to see the phone as well as hear it would make everything easier.

The phone clicked, making the connection, and then smoothly flowed into ringing. It rang once, twice. . . . Another click. Then a gruff voice boomed out of the phone: "Federal Bureau of Investigations. Reardon speaking."

Jonah stabbed his finger at the button to break the connection.

FIVE

"What'd you do that for?" Chip demanded.

"I—I don't think this is the right way to do this," Jonah said. "Sneaking around, looking at papers your parents don't want you to see, calling people . . . I know you're really mad at your parents right now—okay, fine. I don't blame you. But this isn't going to help. Calm down, let them calm down, wait until you can all sit down and talk about it. . . ."

Chip shoved hard against Jonah's chest, pushing him away. The phone fell to the floor between them.

"I don't know what your parents are like," Chip said harshly. "But if my dad says he doesn't want to talk about something, he . . . doesn't . . . talk!" He grabbed the phone and began punching numbers again.

Okay, so maybe family therapist was out as a future career option for Jonah.

"Maybe you should talk to one of the counselors at school or something," Jonah said.

Chip kept punching numbers, stabbing them even harder now.

"I'm not crazy!" he insisted.

"I never said you were," Jonah countered. He guessed Chip had hit about five of the seven numbers for James Reardon now. "But tell me—what do you think the FBI has to do with your adoption?"

Chip stopped hitting numbers.

Jonah eased the phone out of Chip's hands. He pressed the button to hang up.

"Think about it," Jonah said. "This Reardon guy probably doesn't have anything to do with you. That Post-it must have been on some other paper in there. Maybe . . . Is your dad a spy or something?"

"He's a stockbroker," Chip muttered. He cleared his throat. "If he was a spy, he'd probably be on the terrorists' side."

"Maybe he's secretly working for the government," Jonah said. "Maybe he's like a double agent, and he's pretending to launder money for some terrorists, but really he's reporting everything to the government. And maybe if you call this number and blow his cover, like, five years of secret-agent work will go to waste, and they'll have to start all over again. And it will all be your fault."

Jonah had seen a movie once where something like that happened.

"You think my dad's a hero?" Chip asked. "Fat chance."

But he didn't grab the phone back to begin dialing again. He just stood there, looking lost.

"I just want to know who I really am," Chip said. His words came out as a whimper, the kind of sound no self-respecting thirteen-year-old boy would want anyone to hear him making.

Jonah decided not to make fun of him for it.

"I do, too," Jonah said.

"You do?" Chip asked, and this, too, came out sounding pitiful.

Jonah nodded.

"Well, yeah. I mean, my parents are okay, and I guess it'd be *possible* to have a worse sister than Katherine. But sometimes I wonder . . . who do I look like? Are my birth parents good people who just kind of made a mistake? Or are they druggies, alcoholics, criminals . . . are they in jail? Mental hospitals? Did they have any other kids besides me? Did they—did they keep the other kids?"

Sometimes Jonah's mom would say things like, "You have such great dimples and such beautiful eyes—do you suppose those came from your birth mother or your birth father?" Or, "You're so good at math—wonder who you inherited that from?" It annoyed him, because he knew those lines came straight out of the adoption books. And, generally, people whose lives were going great—NFL quarterbacks, rock stars, famous actors and actresses, genius scientists—generally, they didn't give up their kids for adoption. What bad things had he inherited along with the eyes and the dimples and the ability to glide through seventh-grade math?

Chip was nodding.

"Monday morning," he said in a hoarse voice. "When I walked into school, I kept looking around thinking, 'I could have a brother or sister here, and I wouldn't even know it.' So I stared at everyone, looking for curly hair and long skinny legs and nostrils that flare out a little. . . ."

"Is that why you walked into that wall, on the way to lunch?" Jonah asked.

"Uh, yeah," Chip said. He sounded embarrassed.

Jonah eased the Post-it note out of Chip's hand. He waved it slightly in front of Chip's eyes.

"This isn't any good," Jonah said. "No matter what, you're always going to have more questions."

"How do you know?" Chip challenged him. "Have you ever tried to get your questions answered?"

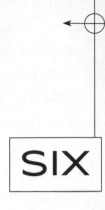

SIX

It was Cincinnati chili night. Mom liked to have themed dinners every so often, and lately she'd been on a geographic kick: spicy New Orleans jambalaya one week, thick New England clam chowder the next, authentic (she said) Mexican hot tamales the next. At least Cincinnati chili was fairly normal, though Jonah failed to see the point of putting chili on top of spaghetti, when Ragú worked just as well.

"Do you think . . . ," he started to say, but everyone was passing around the containers of shredded cheese and chopped onions, and no one seemed to hear him.

A few minutes later, while Katherine was chewing and actually had her mouth shut for once, he tried again.

"You know how you always said that if . . ."

Katherine finished chewing.

"Oh, I almost forgot!" she exploded. "Guess who says she's trying out for cheerleader next year?"

"Do you mind?" Jonah asked. "I was talking first."

Katherine took a gulp of milk.

"Okay, okay, go on," she said. "But hurry up, because this is really funny!"

"All right," Jonah said with injured dignity. "What I was saying was . . . I mean . . ." He swallowed hard.

"Would you just spit it out?" Katherine demanded.

Jonah glared at his sister. He could hear Chip's question echoing in his head: *Have you ever tried to get your questions answered?*

"What was the name of the adoption agency where you, you know, got me?" he blurted.

For a moment, it felt like he'd thrown a grenade out into the center of the table. Even Katherine was speechless for once. Then Mom smiled.

"We've told you that before, but I guess you forgot," she said. "It was called 'Hope for Children.' Awfully schmaltzy, I know, but it felt right to us then, because we had so much hope—and that was all we had. Until—"

"Okay," Jonah said quickly, because he could tell she was about to launch into the miracle story (*the call out of the blue . . . the week before Christmas . . . everything we ever wanted . . .*). He didn't have the patience for that right now, not when he had so much to think about. Hope for Children was a stupid name, but he was relieved, somehow, that it wasn't the Happy Family Adoption Agency, the same one that Chip's family had dealt with. This made the matching letters about being one of the missing seem more like a coincidence, more like an ordinary seventh-grade prank.

Dad was wiping his mouth with his napkin.

"Was there anything else you wanted to know, Jonah?" he asked in a voice that was trying way too hard to sound casual. It was almost as bad as the time Dad had said, on a fishing trip, "You know you can ask me anything you want about puberty."

"Um . . . ," Jonah couldn't decide.

"Can we talk about something that isn't ancient history?" Katherine interrupted.

"Katherine, wait your turn," Mom said. "Jonah?"

Across the table, Katherine crossed her eyes and stuck out her tongue. Jonah looked down at his plate.

"Well, I kind of wondered, now that I'm older, if there's any more information they could give us about, uh, my birth parents," Jonah said. "I mean, not that it really matters. I'm just curious, like—did either of them have dimples? Like me?"

"Dimples!" Katherine snorted indignantly.

Mom shot her one of those looks that said, as clear as

day, *If I hear one more word out of you, young lady, before you have permission to speak, I will cover your mouth with duct tape for the rest of the night.* Of course, Mom had never done anything like that, but her looks always made you believe that she might.

Dad very, very carefully laid his fork on his plate.

"I can certainly call the agency and see if there's any more information available," he said. "But I have to warn you, it's not likely. They weren't even willing to give us a medical history."

"Not that we minded," Mom added quickly. "We were just happy to get you!"

Now Mom and Dad were both beaming at him, stereo smiles. Jonah kicked Katherine under the table.

"Tell your stupid cheerleader story," he muttered.

Later that night, while Jonah was sitting at his desk doing his social studies homework, Katherine shoved her way into his room.

"Don't do this," she said, standing dramatically in his doorway.

"What? Social studies?"

Katherine cast a glance over her shoulder. She stepped aside and eased the door shut behind her. Then—almost cautiously, for her—she sat down on the edge of his bed.

"No, you know," she said. "That whole adopted-kid search-for-identity thing."

Jonah pressed his pencil down too hard on the *sapiens* part of *homo sapiens*, and the lead snapped. He dropped the pencil and whirled around.

"What's it to you?" he asked.

"Hey, I'm part of this family too," Katherine said.

"No, duh." He thought about snarling, *Of course you are. You're actually related by blood. You belong more than I do.* But that wasn't a very Jonah thing to say. It was like all those cruel things Chip had been saying about his dad all afternoon, that were just Chip being mad and surely couldn't be true. He decided to stick with "No, duh," as his best comeback.

Katherine rolled her eyes.

"Look," she said. "It makes them mental, every time you bring up the adoption, or your birth parents, or anything like that. They start pussyfooting around and being so careful, like, 'Now, Jonah . . .'" She'd dropped her voice an octave, in a pretty decent imitation of Dad. "'. . . I can certainly call the agency. . . . We'll do anything we can. . . . We would never want your adoption to impede your self-actualization. . . .'"

Whoa—where had Katherine learned a term like *self-actualization*?

"So what?" Jonah said. "And why's it my fault? They're the ones who always bring up the story of how they got me. 'Blah, blah, blah, call out of the blue . . . blah, blah, blah, blinding rainstorm the night we picked you up . . .'"

Katherine giggled. Then she leaned forward, her eyes round and earnest.

"Yeah, but see, that's the *past*," she said. "That's the beginning of the story of them having kids. It's their story *with* you. It's like them telling about giving me Barbie stickers to get me potty-trained. Or telling about the time I threw up into Mom's purse."

Jonah snorted, remembering. That had been funny.

Katherine eyed him suspiciously.

"You haven't told anybody at school those stories, have you?" she asked.

"No—why would I? Who cares?"

Katherine nodded approvingly.

"You better not," she said. She glanced toward the door once more. "When you start talking about wanting to know more about your birth parents, that's different. You know what they're doing down there right now, don't you? They're reading those books again." Jonah didn't have to ask which ones she meant. "They're trying to figure out what they're supposed to say so you don't start acting out and using drugs and flunking out as your cry for help."

Jonah realized that Katherine had probably read *Raising*

the *Well-Adjusted Adopted Child* and *Adoption Without Secrets* too.

"I'm not going to do any of that stuff," Jonah said. "That's crazy."

"Yeah, well, so's getting all worried about your birth parents. Because, Jonah"—Now she was leaning so far forward, she was only inches from falling off the bed—"your birth parents don't matter. You're Jonah. They could have dimples or they could have three eyes apiece and six fingers on every hand, and it doesn't change a thing about you."

Jonah kind of thought that might be impossible—twelve-fingered, three-eyed parents having a ten-fingered, two-eyed kid—but he wasn't sure. Genetics had never been a big interest for him.

"That's easy for you to say," he muttered in a huff. "You can look in a mirror and know exactly where everything came from. Eyes—brown like Mom's. Nose—ski slope, like Dad's."

"I do not have a ski-slope nose!" Katherine protested. "It's . . . classical."

She turned sideways, as if modeling.

"Classical ski slope maybe," Jonah said.

"It is not! Er—never mind." Katherine waved her hands in front of her face, like she was trying to erase the nose debate. This was a miracle—Katherine backing away from an argument? "What I meant to say is, that doesn't matter either. If you're going through some adolescent 'Who am I?' phase, it's not because you're adopted. *Everyone* goes through that. I don't know who I am either."

Jonah reached out and tapped her on the arm.

"Katherine Marie Skidmore, remember?" he said. "Daughter of Michael and Linda. Granddaughter of—"

"No, no, who am I really?" Katherine interrupted. "Like, next year when we can try out for things, do I want to be a cheerleader or a basketball player? Do I want people to think, 'Katherine Skidmore, airhead, but what a hottie,' or, 'Katherine Skidmore, what a jock!'?"

Jonah was torn. He wanted to tease, *Regardless, it'll be, 'airhead, definitely not a hottie.'* But he also kind of wanted to offer some profound big-brotherly advice along the lines of, *Katherine, you idiot, it's what you are that matters, not what people think you are.* He was saved from making a decision because someone knocked on his door just then. Both he and Katherine jumped guiltily.

"Is this a private party, or are adults allowed too?" Mom called from the hallway.

Katherine shot Jonah a glance that said, *See, I told you they're acting mental.*

Jonah frowned back at her and called out, "Come in" to his mother.

Mom pushed open the door, but still stood there a little hesitantly.

"That Cincinnati chili took so long to make—chopping all those onions!—I totally forgot . . . you got some mail today, Jonah," she said, holding out a white envelope.

Jonah felt a nervous twitch in his stomach.

Mom walked across the room and laid the envelope on his desk, beside his social studies book. Once again, there was no return address. It was just a plain ordinary unmarked letter addressed to Jonah.

"If that's an invitation to a birthday party or some other event you want to go to, let me know so I can put it on the calendar," Mom said, still in that unnatural, careful voice she'd used at dinner.

"Okay. I will," Jonah said.

He made no move to open the letter. He didn't even touch it. He bent his head over his social studies book like the most dedicated student in the world—*Look, Mom! I'm not in any danger of flunking out!*—but he could feel Mom and Katherine both staring at him. He sighed.

"I'll look at it later, okay? I've really got to finish this social studies. We've got a test tomorrow, and I haven't even done the whole study sheet yet," Jonah hinted.

"Oh! All right. Come on, Katherine, we're being kicked

out," Mom said. "Jonah, let me know if you want any help reviewing later."

Jonah waited until they were both gone, and the door was firmly latched. He picked up the envelope and went over to sit on the floor with his back pressed against the door, so he'd have some warning if anyone tried to come in. Carefully, he eased his finger under the flap of the envelope and gently lifted it.

He could tell even before he pulled the letter out that most of it was blank. He fumbled unfolding it, one edge of the paper getting stuck against the other side. And then it was open. He flattened the paper against the floor, so he could see every word all at once.

There were seven this time:

BEWARE! THEY'RE COMING BACK TO GET YOU.

SEVEN

"You didn't tell anyone?" Chip asked.

"I just told you, didn't I?" Jonah said.

"No, I mean, like, a grown-up. Your parents."

Jonah shrugged miserably. They were at the bus stop, but standing apart from the other kids, out of the glow of the streetlight. It was the next morning, and he'd just quietly filled Chip in on the contents of his latest letter.

"What am I supposed to say?" Jonah asked, twisting his face into an imitation of a terrified little kid and making his voice come out high and squeaky: "Oooh, Mommy, Daddy, that piece of paper scared me." He dropped his voice back to its normal register. "Katherine thinks they're freaking out anyhow, just 'cause I asked a few questions last night."

Chip glanced away, and Jonah followed his gaze. In

the darkness, the other kids were mostly miscellaneous blobs, but Jonah could pick out Katherine's bright orange jacket in the middle of a huge cluster of kids. It sounded like she was competing with her friends Emma and Rachel to see who could squeal the loudest.

"Maybe Katherine's the one who sent that letter," Chip said. "I didn't get one. Maybe she's just playing a trick on you—remember, she wanted to rewrite that letter on Saturday, to make it a better prank."

Jonah thought about how serious Katherine had looked the night before, commanding, "Don't do this," how desperately she seemed to want him and his parents to just act normal.

"No," he said curtly. "It's not Katherine."

"Well, then . . . what did the letter say again, exactly?" Chip asked.

"*Beware! They're coming back to get you,*" Jonah recited tonelessly. It took no effort to remember; he'd stared at the words for so long the night before that it seemed like they were imprinted on his eyeballs.

"'Coming back to get you,' huh? Maybe it doesn't have anything to do with your, uh, adoption," Chip said. Jonah noticed Chip was still having trouble making himself say the word. "Maybe it's a revenge thing. Have you made anybody mad lately?"

You, Jonah thought, but didn't say. He couldn't blame Chip any more than he blamed Katherine.

"I'm sure it's just another prank," Jonah said, but he wasn't sure. If anything, he was almost sure that it wasn't.

The school bus appeared out of the early-morning darkness just then, and he and Chip crammed themselves into the screaming, squealing line of kids jabbering about how Spencer Patton was going to sneak his iPod into math class today and how Kelly Jefferson had just broken up with Jordan Cowan and, "Did you hear—six kids got sick from eating the cafeteria pizza yesterday! Do you think they'll finally fire the lunch ladies?" Jonah hoped that no one could tell that he felt like he was walking around in a bubble. Even as he climbed up the bus steps, walked down the crowded aisle, and collapsed into the first vacant seat, he felt like he was in a completely different dimension from kids who cared about iPods and math class and breakups and cafeteria pizza.

Two stupid letters—thirteen stupid words, total—and I'm freaking out? I'm as bad as Mom and Dad!

First period was study center, and he forced himself to look over his social studies notes. He studied so hard that, second period, the test was a breeze. He filled in the meaningless words—*Homo erectus, Homo habilis, Homo sapiens, Neanderthal*—with great relief. These, at least, were questions he could answer. He turned in his paper feeling confident that he'd gotten everything right, even the bonuses.

See, Katherine, I am not going to flunk out as a cry for help! he thought. *That's going to be my best test grade all year!*

Some of the other kids evidently weren't so happy.

"Come on, Mr. Vincent," Spencer Patton said. "Even you've got to admit this stuff is stupid. Why do we have to study history anyway?"

"So you know where you come from," Mr. Vincent said.

I wish, Jonah thought.

"And—Oh! I know!—it'll help if anyone ever invents a time machine," Jeremy Evers wisecracked. "This way, when you go back in time, you can recognize people, so you'll know who you've got to speak Neanderthal to, and who just uses regular caveman talk."

"Very funny, Jeremy," Mr. Vincent said in a tone that didn't sound amused. "Let's stay within the realm of reality, shall we?"

The realm of reality—Jonah liked that term. He imagined telling Mr. Vincent about the letters, and having Mr. Vincent shake his head dismissively and say, "Come on, Jonah. Stay within the realm of reality." Reality was supposed to be social studies tests and cafeteria pizza, not strange letters and worrying that someone was going to snatch him away, worrying that he'd made a big mistake not telling Mom and Dad about the letters and having them taken to the police to be fingerprinted. . . .

What am I thinking? Mom and Dad would laugh their heads off, me acting like they should report some seventh-grade prank to the police!

Mr. Vincent called on Jonah to answer a question, and Jonah didn't even know what he'd asked.

The rest of Jonah's day went like that too. In science class he dropped a test tube full of a liquid that tested as strongly acidic. (It turned out that it was only lemon juice, but his lab partner still got mad that he'd splashed it on her Abercrombie & Fitch top.) In gym class he got hit on the head with a volleyball. In band he miscounted the rests and came in at the wrong time, the only trumpet playing in a measure that was supposed to be all flutes. It was like he'd used up all his focus on the social studies test. He was glad when school was finally over, so he'd be able to go home and plop down in front of the TV, and nobody would notice that he wasn't paying attention.

But as Jonah stepped down from the school bus that afternoon, the last one off, he heard Chip say in a tense voice, "Come with me."

"Huh?" Jonah said, feeling dazed. He hadn't even

noticed that Chip was right in front of him. Had he accidentally agreed to help Chip unlock more safes, sort through more records? Had he even spoken to Chip since this morning at the bus stop?

"Just to my mailbox," Chip said.

Jonah stopped in the street and squinted at him stupidly.

"You know how you can mail two letters from the same mailbox on the same day, and they might arrive wherever they're going on different days?" Chip asked. "Even if where they're going is just two different mailboxes on the same street?"

Comprehension flowed over Jonah.

"You're scared you might get the letter today," Jonah said. "The same letter I got yesterday."

"Not *scared*," Chip corrected quickly. "I mean, if you're busy, I can get the mail by myself. It's just—you're used to being adopted, and you laugh things off, but this is all new to me, you know?"

Oh, yeah, Jonah thought. *This day's been a bundle of laughs.* But he silently turned and followed Chip toward the mailbox at the end of Chip's driveway.

The Winstons' mailbox was one of the fancier ones on the block. Instead of being on a wooden post, it was on a brick column; at the top, the bricks encircled the entire box in a graceful arc. Dimly, Jonah wondered how the builder had done that, how the flimsy metal mailbox wasn't crushed by the heavy bricks and mortar.

Chip reached into the mailbox and pulled out a thick stack of letters and flyers.

"Bill, bill, ad . . . ," Chip flipped through the stack, sounding more relieved with each letter that *wasn't* a plain envelope addressed to him, without a return address. Jonah noticed that some of the Winstons' letters had those yellow forwarding stickers the post office used when people moved, covering an old address with the new one.

"Wait a minute," Jonah said. "When you got that letter on Saturday, was it forwarded from your old address, or was it this address?"

"I don't know." Chip looked up from his sorting for a moment. "This address, I guess. Why?"

"Oh, good," Jonah said. "That means it could just be kids from school, fooling around. They wouldn't know your old address."

Maybe most of the seventh grade had gotten weird letters like his and Chip's. He should have surveyed everyone he knew, instead of wandering around in a daze.

"But how did they know I was adopted—when I didn't even know?" Chip asked, his voice breaking. He bent his head down over the mail again.

"*Missing* doesn't necessarily mean 'adopted,'" Jonah argued. "Or, maybe there's some list in the school office of which kids are adopted, and somebody hacked into the computer system, and they think it's really funny to . . ."

He stopped because Chip didn't seem to be listening anymore. Chip's face had suddenly gone deathly pale. Slowly, he held up three letters, all of them plain envelopes without return addresses. All of them were addressed to Chip; two of the letters had yellow forwarding labels. One of the labels was peeled back a little, and Jonah could see the words, "Winnetka, Illinois" below.

Winnetka was where Chip used to live.

"You open them," Chip said. "I can't."

Jonah took a deep breath and took the letters from Chip. He ripped them open quickly, the same way he took off Band-Aids.

"*You are one of the missing,*" he read from the first letter. Then, "*Beware! They're coming back to get you.*" And the next one, again, "*Beware! They're coming back to get you.*"

Someone had sent Chip two copies of each letter, one to his old address and one to his new.

"Wow," Jonah said. "Whoever sent these letters really wanted to make sure you got them."

Chip opened his mouth, but it didn't seem like he had

anything to say—it was more like he'd lost the power to control his jaw.

"JO-NAH!" someone shouted far down the block, from the direction of Jonah's house. It was Katherine.

"What?" Jonah shouted back.

"There's a message on the answering machine," Katherine hollered. "Dad wants you to call him right away."

Jonah didn't care about Katherine's big identity crisis—cheerleader versus basketball player?—but, he reflected, she certainly had the lungs of a cheerleader.

And it was such a relief to think that, to think about something ordinary and pointless and annoying, like Katherine.

"Okay!" he yelled back, sounding completely normal.

Chip grabbed Jonah's arm.

"You can use my cell," he said. "Dad just doubled the number of minutes I'm allowed to use. It's a bribe, I guess. Like that's going to make up for keeping a secret for thirteen years? Like it even matters? Like minutes can make up for years? I'm going to go over the limit anyhow. If you don't use my cell phone, I'm just going to have to call some recorded message, leave the phone on for hours. . . ."

Jonah wondered if Chip was going into shock. It seemed a little irresponsible to leave him alone, babbling like that, so he took the cell phone Chip offered him. He punched in Dad's work number.

"Hey, Jonah buddy," Dad said, too heartily, as soon as Jonah said hello. "Did you have a good day at school?"

"I think I got an A on the social studies test," Jonah said, trying to sound however he would normally sound on a normal day.

"Great!" Dad said with way too much enthusiasm.

Neither of them said anything for a moment.

"Well," Dad said. "I called the adoption agency today, just like I promised."

He paused. Jonah could tell he was supposed to say, "Oh, thanks, Dad," or "Really, Dad, you didn't have to do that," or even just, "Yeah?" But Jonah found that his mouth was suddenly too dry to say anything.

"Eva, the social worker who helped us—such a great lady—she's not there anymore," Dad said. "But I talked to another woman, who looked up your file, and . . . Jonah, there *is* new information in your case."

Jonah pressed the cell phone more tightly against his ear. He swayed slightly.

"Oh?" he said, and it took such effort to produce that one syllable.

"A name," Dad said. "The social worker was a little con-fused—she wasn't even sure at first that she was allowed to tell me, but . . . it wasn't one of your birth parents. It was just someone listed as having information about you. A contact person."

"Who was it?" Jonah asked, pushing the words out through gritted teeth.

"Some guy named James Reardon," Dad said. "And—get this—he works for the FBI."

EIGHT

The world spun around Jonah. He clutched the cell phone tight against his ear. Normally he was a big fan of cell phones—it was so frustrating that his parents had decided to buy only one cell phone for him and Katherine to share, which meant that Katherine usually had the cell phone and he got nothing. But right now he wanted something a lot more substantial than a cell phone to hold on to: a phone rooted in concrete, maybe.

He settled for grabbing the Winstons' brick-encased mailbox.

"James . . . Reardon?" he repeated numbly.

"Yeah—have you heard of him?" Dad said, puzzlement creeping into his voice.

Was his name written on a Post-it note stuck to my file? Jonah wanted to ask. *A yellow Post-it note just like the one that was in*

Chip's family's safe, probably stuck on his adoption records? Identical Post-it notes, even though Chip was adopted through a different agency and lived in Illinois his whole life until now?

Jonah felt so dizzy, even solid brick was barely enough to hold him up.

"Jonah?" Dad said, sounding worried now.

Jonah realized he'd probably let a lot of time pass, not answering Dad's question, trying to make his vision stop spinning.

"I'm here," Jonah said. "The phone must have cut out for a minute." If in doubt, blame the technology. He gulped and tightened his grip on the bricks. "This guy . . . what does he know about me?"

"I'm not sure," Dad said. "The social worker said it was highly unusual, the way the name was entered in your file. . . ."

Post-it note, for sure, Jonah thought.

"She offered to call him for us, but she was so scattered I thought it might be better if we met with him ourselves."

Jonah glanced over at Chip, who looked as shell-shocked as Jonah felt. And Chip had heard only Jonah's end of the conversation.

"Would you like me to arrange that, Jonah?" Dad asked, in the same super-patient, super-careful voice that he'd used when Katherine was a toddler throwing temper tantrums.

No, Jonah wanted to say. *Tell him to keep his information to himself. Tell him, if he's not busy hunting down terrorists right now, I'd appreciate him taking care of whoever's sending strange letters to thirteen-year-old boys. Tell him . . .*

"Yes," Jonah said.

NINE

Jonah sat in a molded plastic chair. Mom sat in the chair to his right and Dad in the chair to his left, and Jonah knew that if he gave either of them so much as a flicker of encouragement, they would both start clutching his hands and holding on to him just like they had when they'd walked him to his first day of kindergarten.

Jonah was very careful to keep his hands in his lap, as far as possible from his parents' hands. He kept his eyes trained straight ahead, hoping that the FBI had no way of knowing that he'd once hung up on the man he was waiting to see.

By rights, Jonah thought, Chip should be with Jonah too, waiting in this bland government office to meet with James Reardon. Whatever James Reardon knew about Jonah, he probably knew the same information about Chip. It'd be . . . kinder . . . if they could both get their facts at the same time.

Information . . . facts . . . I just want to know who I am, Jonah thought. *And why I've been getting those letters. Does James Reardon know that? Does he know who Chip is?*

Chip was not sitting in any of the molded plastic chairs near Jonah. Jonah had not been able to figure out any way to convince his parents that his new friend, whom he'd barely known for three months, should be included in this intimate, private moment, when Jonah might be about to learn deep dark secrets about his past.

"Maybe you should just tell them the truth," Chip had suggested, as a last resort, in desperation.

Jonah had considered this for a millisecond.

Telling his parents the truth would require informing them that he'd been involved in breaking into somebody else's safe. And that their new neighbors—whom Mom had taken fresh-baked banana bread to and heartily welcomed to the neighborhood—those same neighbors had been lying to their only son for his entire life. And he'd have to tell them that he was receiving threatening letters, and he believed somebody wanted to kidnap him.

If he told them all that, he wouldn't get to take Chip with him to meet James Reardon. He wouldn't get to go himself. He'd be locked up, either to punish or protect him.

"No," he'd told Chip. "I can't. But I promise, I'll tell you everything this guy says. And then you can get your parents to—"

"My parents aren't talking to me about the adoption, remember?" Chip said harshly. "If *they* won't even talk to me about it, what makes you think they'd take me to the FBI to talk about it?"

So Chip wasn't waiting with Jonah. But there was a fourth person sitting in a molded plastic chair on the other side of Dad: Katherine.

Katherine had thrown a fit when Mom and Dad had told her about the meeting, about how she'd have to be home alone for a little bit while they were away with Jonah.

"We should be home in time for dinner," Mom said. "But if you get hungry without us, there's some of that leftover chili—"

"No," Katherine said.

"Okay, if you don't want chili, there's always—"

"I'm not talking about food," Katherine said irritably. "I mean, no, I'm not staying home alone. I'm going with you."

Mom and Dad exchanged glances.

"Katherine, this doesn't really pertain to you," Dad said. "This is about Jonah—"

"And he's my brother and I'm part of this family too, and doesn't everything that affects him affect me, too?" Katherine had said, sweeping her arms out in dramatic gestures, seeming to indicating a family so broad it could be the whole world.

Funny, Jonah thought. *That's not what she said that time I broke a lamp playing Nerf football in the house.*

The argument about Katherine going or not going had raged through the house for three days. And then, inexplicably, Mom and Dad had given in. Mom and Dad didn't usually cave in to Katherine like that. Jonah wondered what she'd promised in exchange: to clean up the kitchen after dinner every single night for the rest of the school year? To do her homework without complaining ever again? To not have a boyfriend until she went to college?

Something beeped and Jonah jumped. Okay, he was overreacting. It was just Katherine playing Tetris on her cell phone. (*Our* cell phone, he corrected himself.) He felt the annoyance bubbling up, stronger than ever. Here he was, staring at a door that maybe hid all the secrets of his life. And Katherine was just sitting there playing a video game?

The door opened, and a man stepped out. But the man was wearing a gray sweatshirt imprinted with the words *Maintenance Staff*. It was a janitor.

"Hey," he said. "Any of you want something to drink while you're waiting? The vending machine spit out two Mountain Dews, and I only wanted one."

"Jonah likes Mountain Dew," Katherine said, pausing her Tetris long enough to point to her brother.

The janitor held out a green bottle to Jonah.

"You should probably call the vending company," Mom said. "If the machine's malfunctioning like that, maybe next time you'll put your money in and not get anything out. And really . . ." she began fumbling in her purse ". . . we can pay for this bottle, if Jonah's going to drink it. . . ."

"No, no, it's all good," the janitor said. "I've put in money before and gotten nothing back. So this is already paid for. I just don't want it. You enjoy it, kid, okay?" He tossed the bottle lightly to Jonah, and Jonah caught it.

Jonah did like Mountain Dew. At his tenth birthday party, he'd drunk an entire two-liter bottle of it, all by himself, on a dare. And he was thirsty. But something about the whole exchange struck him as weird and fake, like in a soft-drink commercial, where people took one sip and were suddenly dancing and singing and hugging total strangers. Was there a secret camera rolling some-where? Would he be expected to do a testimonial at the end?

There I was, bummed out and a little scared, wondering who I really was, when Buster gave me that Mountain Dew and, whoa, suddenly I realized, it doesn't matter; we're all brothers under the skin. He and the janitor would have their arms around each other's shoulders by then, with a kick line of dancing girls behind them, and birds twittering around their heads, and the dreary waiting room transformed into a lovely meadow. . . .

The janitor disappeared back through the door. So no dancing girls and twittering birds. Mom was still pointlessly reaching into her purse—all because of that "Pay your own way" virtue she and Dad always preached. *You'd think they'd want to emphasize the whole Don't-take-candy-from-strangers message too,* Jonah thought. He stared suspiciously down at the bottle. This Mountain Dew could be poisoned. It could be laced with a dangerous narcotic, and the next thing he knew, he'd be waking up in a dark room, his mouth gagged, his wrists and ankles tied together. Maybe James Reardon was a kidnapper, maybe he was the one who'd been sending Jonah and Chip those weird letters, maybe . . .

Jonah noticed that the cap of the Mountain Dew bottle had never been opened. It was still connected to the ring of plastic below it.

You are so paranoid, he told himself. *The reason Mom and*

Dad aren't suspicious is because there's no reason to be suspicious. You're thirsty; someone was nice enough to give you a Mountain Dew—drink it!

Jonah unscrewed the lid, raised the bottle to his lips, and took a huge gulp. Beside him, Dad patted his leg comfortingly.

Jonah was done with the Mountain Dew by the time the door opened again. This time a man in a suit stood framed in the doorway.

"Mr. and Mrs. Skidmore?" he asked, reaching out to shake hands. "I'm James Reardon. Come on back."

The Skidmores followed Mr. Reardon down a long hallway. The offices on either side of the hallway were dark, with the doors shut, as if everyone else had already left for the day. Mom must have noticed this too because she said, "We really appreciate you staying late to meet with us after my husband and I got off from work. We really could have—"

"It's no problem," Mr. Reardon said. He showed them into the only well-lit office, a large room dominated by a huge desk. He shut the door behind them. "Please, have a seat."

There were only three chairs lined up in front of the desk, so Jonah had to tug a fourth one over from beside a couch at the right side of the room.

Couldn't Katherine have gotten the extra chair? Jonah fumed to himself. *She's the extra person!*

He didn't seem to have any control of his emotions suddenly: he was so mad at Katherine, so annoyed with Mom and Dad for sitting down so obediently in their low chairs and staring up at Mr. Reardon like little kids sent to the principal's office. What he wanted to do was just blurt out, "What do you know about me?"

No, he didn't want to do that. He was too scared about how Mr. Reardon might answer.

Mad, annoyed, scared, confused . . . , Jonah listed to himself. *Want fries with that?*

In spite of himself, Jonah grinned. His brain was a mixed-up, bizarre place, but at least he could amuse himself sometimes.

Mr. Reardon cleared his throat. Jonah stopped grinning.

"I thought it was important to have this meeting," Mr. Reardon said in a smooth, silky voice, looking carefully at Mom, then Dad, then Jonah and Katherine, each in turn. "When you called, Mr. Skidmore, it became apparent to me that information had been released that was, ah, inappropriate."

Dad leaned forward. "You mean—"

Mr. Reardon held up his hand, as if only he was allowed to talk.

"Please, let me finish," he said. "I wanted to meet with you to assure you that we aren't trying to hide any information that you're entitled to. But you must understand the delicacy required in matters of national security. And—"

"Our son's background is a matter of national security?" Mom asked incredulously.

Mr. Reardon glanced away for a second, then locked his gaze on Mom's eyes. This reminded Jonah of a spoof he'd seen once in *MAD* magazine that was supposed to teach kids how to lie convincingly. "Peer deeply into your target's eyes" had been one of the first rules on the list.

"I didn't say that," Mr. Reardon said soothingly, his eyes still fixed on Mom's face. "Of course that's ridiculous. To the best of my knowledge, his actual adoption was a very routine matter. But there were various government agencies involved . . . beforehand . . . and some of us do require a certain level of secrecy, just by the very nature of our work. So, there you have it. Really, you should never have been given my name."

He sat back in his chair, smiling apologetically from across the vast reaches of his desk.

"Let me get this straight," Mom said. "You're saying that the FBI had some connection to Jonah's life before he joined our family—and you're not allowed to tell us what it is? You don't think he has a right to know?"

Some of the politeness had gone out of Mom's voice. "Let me get this straight" was the phrase that she always used with Jonah and Katherine when she thought they were stretching the truth a bit. ("Let me get this straight— you started practicing the trumpet at three thirty, according to the kitchen clock, and it's only three fifty now, but somehow I'm supposed to believe that you practiced for an entire half hour out there in the living room? How could that be?") Normally, Jonah hated that stern tone in Mom's voice, that steely look in her eye. But right now he felt like cheering her on.

"Now, now," Mr. Reardon said, leaning forward again. "I can understand how this might be upsetting to you. That 'FBI' title frightens people sometimes. In many ways, the Immigration and Naturalization Service was more involved. But, alas, secrets are secrets. . . ."

"What are you talking about?" Dad asked. "Immigration and Naturalization . . . are you saying Jonah was born in another country?"

Was that what *Immigration and Naturalization* meant?

"I'm an American!" Jonah blurted out, before he could stop himself.

"Of course you are," Mr. Reardon said. "All your paperwork's in order. At the moment. I checked."

He smiled, but it was a dangerous smile. Jonah couldn't

quite understand what was going on, but maybe that was because he felt so dizzy all of a sudden. And so much of his brain was drowning in thoughts like, *All those times I said the Pledge of Allegiance at school—doesn't that count for anything? And the "National Anthem"—I try to sing it at baseball games; it's not my fault my voice doesn't go that high. . . .*

"Is Jonah—" Dad took a careful breath. "Is he a naturalized American citizen or native born?"

Mr. Reardon shrugged, still smiling.

"Why does it matter?"

"It doesn't . . . when it comes to the love we have for our son," Mom said.

Jonah's stomach began to churn, to match his spinning head. If Mom was going to get all sappy right here in front of Mr. Reardon, Jonah wouldn't be able to take it. For a few seconds, he couldn't even listen. When he forced himself to tune back in, Mom was saying, "But it might matter to Jonah someday. If he was born in another country, he might want to go back and visit; he might want to do projects about that country's history for school. . . ."

Mom's voice cracked on the word *school*, and Jonah decided this was nothing like those times she tried to catch him or Katherine in a lie. Her voice never cracked then.

Mr. Reardon leaned closer. He laid his hands lightly on a closed laptop—the only object on his vast desk—

and moved the right corner ever so slightly forward, as if that microscopic readjustment might align it perfectly with the borders of the desk.

"Let me give you a hypothetical," Mr. Reardon said. "Let's say there was an international baby-smuggling ring. Lots of poor people in developing countries have babies they can't afford; lots of rich Americans want babies they can't have. People get desperate, don't they?"

Jonah saw his mother flinch. Mr. Reardon went on.

"It's a bad mix, desperate rich people who want something that desperate poor people have. Laws are broken; rights are trampled; money changes hands illegally—"

"We've done nothing wrong," Dad said coldly.

"I haven't accused you of anything," Mr. Reardon said. "Guilty conscience?"

Dad gaped at Mr. Reardon and lurched forward in his chair.

"Of course not," he said. "Jonah was adopted through a reputable adoption agency—we had no contact with any smuggling rings! We—we didn't pay anything! Except the regular adoption fee . . . but—but everyone pays that!"

Jonah had never before seen Dad so angry that he actually sputtered. He was usually the calmest person in the family, mild-mannered, like a Clark Kent without any secrets.

Mr. Reardon laughed, as if he thought Dad's reaction was funny.

"We're just talking hypotheticals, remember?"

Dad sat back, but Jonah could tell that it took great effort. Mom reached over and took Dad's hand—Jonah could tell that they were both holding on so tightly that their knuckles turned white.

"So, *hypothetically*," Mr. Reardon continued, "this smuggling ring gets greedy. They take too many risks; they get caught. They always do, in the end. It's a big mess for all the governments involved, all the government agencies involved. Do you extradite the smugglers? Do you deport the babies? You probably should, shouldn't you?" He was staring straight at Jonah now. "*Extradite* and *deport* both mean 'send back,' by the way."

Katherine gasped.

Jonah's stomach was still churning, his head still spinning. But Katherine's gasp was the last straw. He was sick of sitting here listening to Mr. Reardon bully his family with all these "hypotheticals," all these simpers and smirks, cruel smiles and humorless laughs. He hated the way Mom and Dad were clutching each other, terrified, the way even Katherine had all the color drained from her face. If there was any way Jonah could hurry this along, a sick stomach and a whirling head weren't going to stop him.

"Which country was it?" Jonah asked.

"Pardon?" Mr. Reardon asked.

"Which country?" Jonah repeated. "I see where you're going with all this. Some smuggling ring brought me into the United States, the government busted up the smuggling ring, you gave me to a regular adoption agency, and then Mom and Dad got me. I'm really glad you didn't send me back, if it was one of those countries where people live on five dollars a year. But it would be nice to know where I came from. Just so—just to know."

Jonah was amazed at how calm his voice sounded. *Really, who cares?* He thought. He'd always known his DNA came from strangers; did it really matter if they were strangers from Bangladesh or Ethiopia or China instead of Kansas or Kentucky or Maine?

Jonah glanced down and caught a glimpse of his arm: pale skin, light brown hairs, an occasional freckle. Okay, he guessed he couldn't be from Bangladesh or Ethiopia or China. Which poor country had people who looked like him?

It would be nice to know.

"I'm sorry," Mr. Reardon said. He didn't sound sorry at all. "You're asking me for information that I'm not authorized to provide."

"Then—who would be?"

Mr. Reardon shrugged.

"Nobody."

It doesn't matter, Jonah told himself. *I don't care.* But that wasn't true. The room seemed to whirl around him—the room full of lies, Mr. Reardon's lying words, Jonah's lying thoughts. He shook his head dizzily. Mom reached out and placed her hand over his, just as she'd done with Dad.

Jonah didn't shove it away.

"It seems to me," Dad said slowly, "that my son's question is perfectly reasonable." Jonah was relieved to see that Dad had apparently calmed down now or at least was keeping himself under better control. "I don't quite understand the need for all this secrecy. Don't law enforcement agencies usually want to publicize big arrests? Aren't smuggling busts public information?"

"Not always," Mr. Reardon said. "Many times we have strong reasons to keep something like this secret. And I can't tell you the reasons without giving away the secrets. Quite a quandary, isn't it?"

Dad and Mr. Reardon seemed to be staring each other down.

"I understand," Dad said, "that there are ways for American citizens to request information that they believe should be open to the public. My wife and I could make a Freedom of Information request. We could file a lawsuit if we had to. We would be willing to do that, on our son's behalf."

Dad wasn't blinking—but neither was Mr. Reardon.

Jonah was. He was actually scrunching up his entire face, trying to understand. Was Dad threatening to sue? Mom and Dad weren't the type to go around filing lawsuits. They were turn-the-other-cheek types.

"You could do those things," Mr. Reardon agreed, "but you might want to consider your actions very, very carefully. Sometimes there are . . . repercussions. I *think* your son's documentation is in order, but perhaps if we were forced to revisit his case, we might discover some unfortunate discrepancies. Did you hear about the Venezuelan boy who was deported recently? He was only seventeen years old, he'd spent his whole life in the U.S. except for the first three months, he didn't even speak Spanish, but"—another careless shrug—"he wasn't here legally. I'm sure he'll survive in Venezuela somehow."

"Are you threatening us?" Mom asked in a shrill, unnatural voice Jonah was sure he'd never heard her use before. Her hand pressed down on Jonah's. Jonah thought about all those times she'd given him her hand to squeeze when he was a little kid getting shots or that time he had to have sixteen stitches in his knee. Now she was squeezing his hand just as hard. "You couldn't take him away from us. We wouldn't let him go. He's our son!"

"*Is* he?" Mr. Reardon asked. "What if his real parents came forward, wherever they are? What if they told their story?—'Our son, stolen away from us . . .'"

Jonah wanted to correct Mr. Reardon just as he'd corrected Chip: *birth parents, you mean. My real parents are Mom and Dad.* "B—" he started to say. But his churning stomach lurched; he changed his mind about what he wanted to say. "Bathroom," he moaned, his face contorting. "Got to get to the—"

"Oh, for crying out loud!" Mr. Reardon snapped, just as Mom, with much more sympathy, gasped, "Oh, Jonah—maybe the trash can—"

Mr. Reardon reacted as if having a boy vomit in his office would be a form of torture. He sprang up, rushed to the door, flung it open. "There!" he said, pointing down the hall. "Fourth door on the right. Hurry!"

Jonah ran, clutching his stomach. The hallway seemed even longer than it had before. He had a few dry heaves. *Second door. Third door. Here it is, just in time—*

He stumbled into darkness, fumbled for the light, hurried into a stall. All the Mountain Dew he'd drunk came back up, along with the—*never mind,* Jonah told himself. *Don't even try to remember what you had for lunch.*

Then he was done. He leaned his head miserably against the cool metal of the stall.

"Sorry about that," someone said behind him. "It wasn't supposed to make you sick."

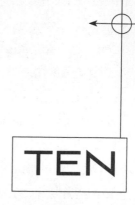

TEN

Jonah spun around—or, spun as well as anyone could, three seconds after vomiting. A man in a gray maintenance-staff sweatshirt stood leaning against the tile wall, but it wasn't the same janitor who'd given him the Mountain Dew. That guy had been older, paunchier. This guy was young and didn't really look like a janitor somehow.

"We've had to do way too much planning on the fly here—we just thought, twenty ounces of Mountain Dew, at some point you'd have to leave that office and go to the bathroom," the man said. "So we could get you alone."

Jonah realized he was practically trapped in the bathroom stall. To get out, he'd have to walk right past the man. Hadn't this day already been horrifying enough? He darted a quick glance down—maybe if he dived fast enough, he could roll out under the wall of the stall and make it to the door out into the hallway before the man saw what he was doing.

The man caught Jonah's glance.

"It's not like that!" the man said, holding up his hands innocently. "I just wanted to tell you something."

"What?" Jonah said, cautiously. Maybe he could swing the stall door into the man's face, maybe he could jump up on the toilet and hang on to the stall's walls to get leverage to kick, maybe—

"When you go back to Mr. Reardon's office," the man said, quickly, like he thought he might run out of time, "find a way to look in the file of papers on his desk. Memorize all the names you can."

"There isn't a file on Mr. Reardon's desk," Jonah said. "Just a laptop."

He was sure of that. He could close his eyes and picture the vast expanse of the desk, almost completely empty.

"There will be when you get back," the man said.

The man took a step toward Jonah, and Jonah tensed. But the man kept going, around the corner of the stall toward the door out into the hallway. Jonah didn't hear the door open and close, but when he peeked out, the man was gone.

Jonah collapsed against the metal stall again. He took a deep breath. *Steady* . . . He found he was clearheaded enough now to remember to flush the toilet.

A pounding noise came from the hallway, somebody pounding on the door.

"Jonah! Jonah, are you all right in there?"

It was Mom, treating him like a kindergartener again.

"I'm fine!" he yelled out.

"Do you need any help?"

"No! Just give me a minute!"

He went to the sink, splashed water on his face, scooped water up into his mouth, and swallowed. His mouth still tasted gross. He leaned his forehead against the mirror.

Papers, he thought. *Look into the file on Mr. Reardon's desk. . . .*

"Jonah?" Mom called from the other side of the bathroom door.

"Coming."

Jonah wiped his face on his sleeve—okay, not good manners, but it was the best he could do under the circumstances—and left the bathroom. Mom was waiting right outside the door; Dad and Mr. Reardon were a little farther down the hall.

"Are you—" Mom started to ask, but Jonah cut her off.

"I told you, I'm okay! Let's just get this over with."

Mr. Reardon watched coldly as Mom and Jonah went back toward his office.

"Really," he said, "I believe we're done here."

"No, no, please—Jonah's fine now," Mom said. "We still need to talk this out. I think we just got off on the wrong foot."

Getting off on the wrong foot was a Mom catchphrase—that was what she'd said about Jonah and Billy Barton in second grade, when Jonah came home with a black eye. (Jonah had completely misunderstood: "No, Mom," he'd insisted, "it was his right fist. Not his foot at all.")

Mr. Reardon looked doubtful, but they all settled back into their chairs near Katherine, who'd evidently never bothered getting up. Jonah shot her a resentful glance, but she looked even worse than he felt: she was deathly pale, and her eyes were huge and round, as if she'd just been terrified out of her wits.

Wow, Jonah thought. *I've never known* Katherine *to be that concerned about me getting sick.*

"I'm fine," he half-whispered, half-mouthed to her. But her eyes stayed huge; her skin stayed pale.

Mr. Reardon and Jonah's parents were still talking, but Jonah tuned it out for a moment. Pretending he was just, oh, maybe trying to see if Mr. Reardon's laptop was a Mac or a PC, he glanced toward Mr. Reardon's desk.

There was a file there now. It was one of those thin, cheap, neutral-colored folders people used in offices.

But at the same time Jonah looked at the folder, Mr. Reardon did too. Jonah was sure he did, even though he didn't move his head at all, and his voice didn't waver. In fact—Jonah started watching Mr. Reardon now—Mr. Reardon kept glancing at the file surreptitiously, every few seconds. It reminded Jonah of the time that he'd broken a window playing baseball, and he'd thought that if he just didn't mention it, maybe Mom and Dad wouldn't notice. But when Dad came out into the backyard, no matter how hard Jonah tried, he couldn't keep from looking toward the broken window. It was like the window was a magnet with an irresistible pull on his eyes.

The file seemed to have the same pull for Mr. Reardon.

Of course, Jonah had been only six years old then, and Mr. Reardon was a grown-up. But the more Jonah ignored what Mr. Reardon was saying (something about the greater good of the entire nation and compromises made by all Americans for the sake of security), and the more he just paid attention to the small twitches of Mr. Reardon's eyes, the more Jonah was sure of three things:

1. Mr. Reardon was surprised and upset—no, make that *furious*—to see that file on his desk.

2. Mr. Reardon really, really, really didn't want Jonah's family to notice the file on his desk.

3. There was no way Jonah would be able to casually lean forward, open the file, then look at and memorize its contents. Not when Mr. Reardon was already alternating his nervous glances at the file with nervous glances at Jonah.

Because I was sick? Because this whole meeting's about me? Or because he already saw me looking at the file?

"Really," Mr. Reardon was saying. "I believe we've already covered this. I see no reason to continue this discussion."

Oh, no! Mr. Reardon was about to end the conversation and kick them out of his office!

Jonah panicked. Should he fake another stomach problem? No—Mom and Dad would focus all their attention on him; it'd just give Mr. Reardon the perfect opportunity to hide the file. What then?

Jonah glanced around frantically, at the ceiling, the floor, the windows behind Mr. Reardon's desk. He glanced back at the floor a second time, at Katherine's red-striped shoelaces flapping out loose and dangling down beside the leg of the chair.

Hmm. Windows. Shoelaces.

Jonah pitched forward.

"Hey, Katherine," he said loudly, "your shoelaces are untied."

For a moment, Jonah was afraid that she wasn't going to react—why was *she* acting so freaky? But then she did lean forward, at least enough so that their heads were below the level of the desk, out of sight. Then Jonah could whisper, directly into her ear, "I'm going to distract Mr. Reardon. Look inside that file on his desk. Memorize as much of it as you can."

Katherine nodded—or, at least, Jonah thought she did. He didn't really have time to make sure. He straightened up.

"Well," Mom was saying, starting to stand up. "We do appreciate you meeting with us, like I said before. But—"

"What's that?" Jonah interrupted, pointing out the window. He sincerely hoped Mr. Reardon had never been a middle-school teacher, because if he had, he'd never fall for this. But Jonah tried not to think about that. He made his voice sound innocent and stunned. "Was that, like, a ball of flame?"

He jumped up and dashed behind Mr. Reardon's desk. This was the risky part. He spun Mr. Reardon's chair around, to face it toward the window.

Katherine—now! He thought. But he couldn't glance

back to make sure she was following instructions. He had to think about his own part.

"Look, Mr. Reardon," he cried. "Can you—" he tried to act as though a horrifying thought had just occurred to him. "—Can you see the airport from here?"

Mr. Reardon did stand up and peer out the window. It was getting dark outside, and the glass was tinted. The only thing Jonah could really see was parking-lot lights. But Jonah hoped it took Mr. Reardon a long time to figure that out.

Mom and Dad were clustered by the window too.

"We *are* awfully close to the airport," Mom murmured. "Oh, those poor people . . ."

Thanks, Mom. Nice touch.

"I don't see anything," Mr. Reardon said. Was there a flicker of suspicion in his voice?

"Maybe we're at the wrong angle," Jonah said. He crouched down a little, pointed. "Over to the right, I think—"

"There's nothing out there," Mr. Reardon said, and he sounded certain now.

"Wow, that's weird," Jonah said. "Are you sure? From where I was sitting, it looked like . . ."

He shouldn't have said, "where I was sitting." Mom, Dad, and Mr. Reardon all turned around, looking toward

Jonah's chair. Fortunately, Katherine wasn't poring over the folder at that moment; she was leaning against the edge of Mr. Reardon's desk closest to the window, her arms behind her, her gaze fixed straight ahead—as if she, too, were engrossed in searching for Jonah's mysterious light.

But how could she possibly have had enough time to look in the folder, memorize whatever was in there, and then position herself in front of the desk?

Jonah's heart sank. His big act had been for nothing.

"I guess—I guess it must have just been a reflection," he said.

Some of the disappointment must have crept into his voice, making it sound like he'd really been hoping to see a dramatic plane crash, because Mom said, a little disapprovingly, "Thank goodness that's all it was."

Then Mr. Reardon was showing them out, down the hallway, through the waiting area, out into the parking lot. Jonah didn't see a single other janitor, with or without Mountain Dew. Jonah held Katherine back as they approached the car, as soon as they were out of Mr. Reardon's view.

"Did you get to see any of those papers?" he whispered.

"Not really," she admitted.

"Thanks a lot," Jonah said bitterly. He knew it wasn't really fair to be mad at her. She hadn't had any time. Still . . .

"I did better than that." Katherine held up the cell phone. "I got pictures!"

ELEVEN

"You have to admit I'm a genius," Katherine said.

"Shh," Jonah hissed.

Mom and Dad were right in front of them, talking in low grim voices, their shoulders hunched over in defeat and dismay.

"No, really," Katherine persisted. "After what I saw, the fact that my brain worked at all is amazing. And then, to think of something like this—"

"Can it, will you?" Jonah interrupted the self-congratulations. "We'll have to talk later. Right now . . ."

Already, Dad was turning around, putting his arm around Jonah's shoulders.

"Jonah, I am so sorry about all of this," he said. "This is not how the government is supposed to work. That man has evidently forgotten that he's supposed to be a servant of the people, that the government is supposed to benefit *us*—"

"Dad, I don't need a civics lesson, okay?" Jonah shrugged away his father's arm.

"That Mr. Reardon needs one," Mom said. "Ooh—I can't remember the last time somebody made me so mad. The nerve! Threatening us . . ." Her voice shook, and she turned quickly away to dab at her eyes.

Jonah slipped into the car. He felt so strange already— the last thing he needed was to watch his parents having emotional breakdowns.

Mom and Dad were getting into the front seat.

Good, Jonah thought. *Just drive away—you'll have to face forward for that. . . .*

But Dad wasn't pushing the key into the ignition. He turned around in his seat and peered earnestly back at Jonah.

"I promise you, Jonah," he said in a husky voice. "If you want us to pursue this, we will. That man had no right to imply that we would be punished for asking questions. You *are* an American citizen. He can't take that away from you."

"Just forget it!" Jonah said harshly. He glanced over at Katherine, on the seat beside him. She was holding out the cell phone.

Names, Jonah thought. *Maybe there's the name of a country.*

Maybe there're the names of a man and a woman. My birth parents.

"You're scared," Dad said. "I understand. You shouldn't make any final decisions right now. Think about it."

"And, Jonah," Mom began, sniffling a little, "if you ever want to just talk things out, we—"

"Can we just do that some other time?" Jonah snapped.

"Sure," Mom said quietly.

A silence enveloped the car. Jonah saw Dad take one hand off the steering wheel and slip it into Mom's hand. But they didn't try to say anything else to Jonah. Dad pulled out of the parking lot and was quickly out on the highway. The streetlights and the lights of passing trucks and cars flashed intermittently into the car.

Jonah reached for the phone in Katherine's hand.

When they'd first gotten the phone, he'd spent about an hour taking pictures of wacky things—his big toe peeking out of his holey sneakers, the dust bunnies under his bed, a close-up of his guinea pig's eye. But he hadn't played with the camera much since then. It seemed to take him forever to navigate from *Menu* to *Camera* to *Saved Pix*.

The first picture he clicked on was just a blur.

"Couldn't you have held it steady?" he whispered to Katherine.

She took the phone away from him. "There!" she said, and handed it back.

The phone's screen was so tiny, it was hard to read anything. But Jonah could make out one line, a title at the top of an infinitesimally small list.

The title wasn't *Birth Parents* or *Country of Origin*.

It was *Witnesses*.

TWELVE

"Download it all," Jonah said. "Hurry."

He and Katherine were at Chip's house, because Chip's computer was in the basement, not right smack in the middle of the kitchen, where anyone could see. (Mom and Dad believed all those warnings about how kids shouldn't have privacy online.) Jonah and Katherine had brought the cell phone and a cable with them, and Katherine was convinced that as soon as they got the pictures on the computer screen, everything would be big and clear and easy to read.

They were still trying to explain to Chip what they were about to show him.

"Didn't this Reardon dude have a copier?" Chip asked. "Or a printer? Couldn't he have printed you an extra copy, instead of making you take pictures?"

"No, no," Jonah said. "Mr. Reardon didn't give this to us."

"He wouldn't tell us squat," Katherine agreed. "The file of papers came from a ghost."

"What?" Jonah and Chip both said, almost exactly at the same time. Jonah glared at his sister, and added, "So help me, Katherine, this is all weird enough. If you think it's funny to just make stuff up—to, to make fun of me—"

"I'm not making anything up!" Katherine said, her eyes wide and innocent. "Honest! That's what I was trying to tell you before, why I was so scared. Didn't you wonder how the file ended up on Mr. Reardon's desk in the first place?"

Jonah hadn't thought to wonder that. There hadn't been time.

"Wasn't it one of the janitors—?" he began.

"Only if the janitors there have supernatural powers."

"Katherine!" Jonah complained.

"Really!" Katherine said. "When you went off to throw up—"

"You threw up?" Chip asked, intrigued.

"Too much Mountain Dew," Jonah said quickly, to make it clear that it hadn't been from nerves or anything like that.

"Anyhow," Katherine continued, "I looked away from

the hallway because I didn't want to see anything gross. And then, right before you came back, this man just . . . appeared. He was right beside Mr. Reardon's filing cabinet. He took out the file, put it on Mr. Reardon's desk, and then he just . . . vanished."

"Maybe you blinked," Jonah said. "Twice." There was a cruel edge to his voice. He didn't need this. Not when he was already stressed out about what he was about to see on the computer screen.

"I didn't blink," Katherine said indignantly. "I know what I saw."

"What did the ghost look like?" Chip asked. "Kind of wavery and see-through?"

Amazing. He sounded like he was taking Katherine seriously.

"Maybe a little bit," Katherine said, tilting her head to the side thoughtfully. "I mean, I didn't have time to look at him closely. He was wearing a gray sweatshirt and jeans but he didn't look scruffy at all." She giggled a little. "Really, he was kind of cute."

"Brown hair?" Jonah asked. "Cut short? And greenish eyes, with kind of crinkles around them?"

Katherine nodded.

"That was the guy from the bathroom, then, the one who told me about the file," Jonah said. "You just, I don't know, missed seeing him walk into and out of the room."

Katherine narrowed her eyes.

"Did Mom and Dad see him?" she challenged.

Jonah hadn't thought of that.

"Give me that phone," he said, reaching for the cell.

"It's still downloading—here." Chip handed Jonah the cordless phone he'd used before, to call Mr. Reardon.

Jonah began carefully dialing their home number. Mom answered.

"You and Katherine will be home soon, won't you?" she asked anxiously. "It's getting late."

"Sure," Jonah said. "Soon. We're just working on a . . . project." He swallowed hard. "Hey, Mom, you know, this afternoon when I was, um, throwing up? Did you see any-one walk out of the bathroom and into Mr. Reardon's office?"

"No," Mom said. "Except for you. Why?"

"Katherine thought that—"

Katherine glared at him. Jonah decided to try another approach.

"I thought I heard, um, footsteps," Jonah said. "Like there was somebody else in the bathroom with me. But then when I came out of the stall, there wasn't anybody else there."

Incredibly, that was almost entirely the truth.

"Was there maybe another door into and out of the bathroom?" Mom asked.

"No."

"Well, then, you must have been imagining those footsteps, because I was standing out in the hall the whole time," Mom said. "And I didn't see anyone come out of that bathroom besides you."

Jonah thought about this. It didn't make any sense.

"Did Dad see anyone?" he asked.

"Jonah, if I didn't see anyone, how could Dad have seen anyone? There wasn't anybody there!" Mom didn't usually get so impatient. Jonah could tell by her tense tone of voice that she was still upset from the meeting with Mr. Reardon. "Why does it even matter?"

"Never mind," Jonah said.

He hung up. Chip and Katherine were staring at him.

"There must have been a secret passageway or something," he said stubbornly. "Like, underground."

"Oh, and you think I would have missed noticing if this guy came up out of a secret underground passage?" Katherine asked sarcastically.

Jonah shrugged. He didn't think he could have missed noticing a secret passageway in the bathroom either. But he wasn't going to admit that to Katherine.

"The pictures are ready on the computer," Chip announced.

Jonah was glad of the distraction.

The first photo that came up was lips.

"Oops—that's from Rachel's sleepover," Katherine apologized. "Molly kissed the phone. She wanted to see what her lip print looked like."

"Girls really do stuff like that?" Chip asked, looking stunned.

Jonah thought Chip needed a sister of his own, so he'd know how stupid and disgusting it all was.

Katherine skipped ahead through the pictures. She stopped on the first shot full of words.

"*Witnesses*," it said at the top. Then, below, "*Angela DuPre, 812 Stonehenge Court, (513) 555-0184 . . .*"

"You only got one of the names?" Jonah complained.

"The rest is in the next shot," Katherine said. "I was trying to follow a pattern, six shots per page, right side, then left side, then down. . . ."

Jonah supposed he really should be impressed, that Katherine could have been so methodical only moments after seeing what she thought was a ghost. But he certainly wasn't going to tell her that.

Katherine's angles were a little off, so she'd gotten only two shots with complete names and addresses and phone numbers, and two other witness names that could be pieced together from multiple shots.

Jonah felt a wave of disappointment.

"What good does this do?" he asked. "These people could be witnesses to *anything*. They probably don't have any connection to me, except that some strange guy in a bathroom wanted to mess with my mind."

"No," Chip said. "Take a look at this."

Chip had sat down at the computer and was manipulating the images, piecing several photos together like a jigsaw puzzle.

The second sheet of paper in the folder hadn't been titled *Witnesses*. It'd been titled *Survivors*. And the last two names on the list were very familiar:

JONAH SKIDMORE
CHIP WINSTON

THIRTEEN

"Close it down," Jonah said.

"Wha-why?" Chip asked.

Jonah stepped back from the computer, far enough away that the words were just indistinct squiggles.

"I don't want to know anything else," he said.

He felt overwhelmed suddenly, everything catching up with him at once: the strange letters, Mr. Reardon implying he could lose his citizenship and be deported, Katherine claiming she'd seen a ghost, and now these lists of witnesses and survivors—with Jonah's name right there in black and white. It made everything else seem like it might be real.

"Can't we go back to, 'Hey, Jonah, you gonna try out for the basketball team?'" Jonah pleaded. "Like that's the most important thing?"

Chip and Katherine were staring at him like he'd completely lost it.

"Can't we pretend none of this ever happened?" Jonah asked.

"My parents spent thirteen years pretending nothing ever happened," Chip said in a hard voice.

Jonah appealed to Katherine.

"You're the one who said I shouldn't do this whole identity-search thing," he said. "You wanted me to just act normal."

Katherine looked from Jonah to Chip and back again.

"That was before I saw the ghost," she said quietly. "Or whatever it was."

"Aren't you curious?" Chip asked.

Jonah shook his head.

"No," he said. "Not at all." He felt like he was still too close to the computer screen. His mind kept trying to turn the vague squiggles back into words and words into ideas. *Survivors. I'm on the survivors list. What does that mean?* He reminded himself that he didn't care. He bent over and picked up his jacket. "Come on, Katherine. Let's go home."

Katherine didn't move.

"I used to want to be you," she said.

"Excuse me?" Jonah asked, almost dropping his jacket in surprise.

"Er—not really *you*," Katherine said. "I wanted to be the one who was adopted. I thought it was so boring to have Mom and Dad as my real parents *and* birth parents. I used to pretend that I was adopted, and that my other parents were a king and a queen, or actors or singers, or— something exciting like that."

"Very nice," Jonah said sarcastically. "I'm sure that little fantasy made you very happy." His hands shook as he pulled on his jacket. He stuffed them into his pockets. "My other parents are probably drug dealers," he said. "Smugglers. Wanted by the FBI."

Katherine shook her head.

"You don't know that," she said.

"Mr. Reardon does." No matter how hard he tried, Jonah couldn't keep the bitterness out of his voice.

"No." Katherine was staring at him. "I don't think so," she said slowly. "Didn't you see how Mr. Reardon was looking at you? It was like . . . like he was trying to figure you out. Like he doesn't really know who you are either."

"Thanks a lot," Jonah said. "Is that supposed to make me feel better?"

Katherine put her hand dramatically on Jonah's arm.

"Wait," she said. "I think I just figured something out."

Jonah waited. *How stupid am I*, he thought, *that I'm obeying Katherine?*

"Okay, okay, I really think I'm right about this," Katherine said excitedly. "See, part of my deal with Mom and Dad, to get to go to the FBI with you, was that I wasn't allowed to say anything while we were there."

"They actually thought you could go three seconds without talking?" Jonah asked.

"I *didn't* talk," Katherine said indignantly.

Jonah considered this. He hadn't noticed at the time, but now that he thought about it, he couldn't remember Katherine saying anything in Mr. Reardon's office. Just gasping.

"And, it's kind of funny," Katherine went on, "but when you're not talking, sometimes you notice things more. And I kept thinking that Mr. Reardon was acting weird."

"No, duh," Jonah said.

Katherine ignored him.

"I kept thinking, why'd he agree to meet with us just to tell us he couldn't tell us anything? And I think"—she dropped her voice low, conspiratorially—"I think it was because he wanted to find out what Mom and Dad already knew."

"You mean, he thought your family knew something that the FBI didn't?" Chip asked. He'd spun around from the computer screen and was staring up at Katherine as if she had all the answers.

"Maybe," Katherine said, back to her normal voice. "Or he was afraid that we already knew some of that top-secret information he didn't want anyone to know. Didn't you notice how it was almost like he was *trying* to get Mom and Dad mad? You know how, when people are mad, sometimes they say things they don't mean to—they reveal too much? That's what Mr. Reardon wanted Mom and Dad to do."

Chip was squinting at Katherine.

"How does that explain the ghost?" he asked.

"*That* I haven't figured out yet," Katherine said with a little laugh. "But I will."

She made this whole mess sound as if it was just a challenging math problem, or as if she was working on a scheme to get Mom and Dad to let her stay up late on a school night or have nothing but ice cream for dinner. This was just an intriguing puzzle to her. It wasn't *her* life.

"Whatever," Jonah said, jerking his arm away from Katherine's grasp. "You can stay here until you figure everything out. I'm going home."

He half-expected Katherine to follow him out—she was *his* sister, after all, not Chip's friend—but when he glanced back, they'd both turned around to huddle over the computer together.

Fine, Jonah thought. *See if I care.*

When he'd climbed up the stairs to the first level of Chip's house, he could hear a TV siren blaring from the family room. A woman—presumably Chip's mom—said unhappily, "You always have to watch the blood-and-guts shows." Jonah thought about walking back toward the family room, poking his head in, and informing Chip's parents, "You really ought to know what's going on, down in your basement. Chip's looking for a whole other identity that doesn't involve you." Instead he turned through the dark dining room and slipped out the front door.

Outside, a new thought occurred to him. Chip had pretty much admitted that he had a crush on Katherine— what if Katherine had a crush on Chip, too? What if *that's* what this was all about?

Unaccountably, Jonah suddenly felt very lonely. He was walking down a dark street, all by himself, the trees casting eerie shadows across the sidewalk. *Hey, kidnappers,* he thought, *you want to get me back? This would be a great time to snatch me away!*

He shivered, even though it wasn't the least bit cold for October.

I should have told Mom and Dad, he thought. *About that second letter, if nothing else.*

But he knew why he hadn't. They would have made a federal case out of it, getting upset, calling the cops . . . Jonah didn't want that. Like Katherine, he wanted Mom and Dad to stay normal. And now he really couldn't tell them, not when they were already so freaked out by the meeting with Mr. Reardon. It would be cruel to spring this on them too.

The street curved slightly, and there was a break in the trees, so he had a full view of his own house. Mom had chrysanthemums planted along the sidewalk and along the front fence—which was actually white picket. Mom and Dad were such believers in all those cliches. The living room bay window curved out invitingly, the lights blazed . . . home looked like such a safe place. Jonah just wanted to walk in, crawl into bed, pull the covers over his face, and sleep until all the scary things in his life disappeared.

He glanced longingly up at the two second-story windows that looked into his room. The lights weren't on in his room, but light was spilling in from the hallway, so he could make out dim shapes: his dresser, his desk, the posts of his bed. . . .

One of the shapes in his room moved.

While Jonah watched, a dark shape—no, a *person*—eased the door of Jonah's room shut, blocking out the light, plunging the windows into complete darkness. But then a smaller light—a flashlight? a penlight?—clicked on, hovering over Jonah's desk.

Jonah took off running.

FOURTEEN

Jonah burst in through the front door.

"Mom? Dad?" he called accusingly. If they were snooping in his room, he was going to be really angry. He hadn't started flunking out of school as a cry for help—there was no reason for them to search through his things.

Mom peeked out from the kitchen, drying her hands on a dish towel.

"Dad and I are back here," she said.

Jonah sped around the corner, saw Dad sitting at the computer. Dad hastily clicked out of whatever he was looking at, but not before Jonah caught a glimpse of the FBI crest—*Thanks, Dad, you really think you have to hide that from me?* Jonah decided he didn't have time to think about that right now.

"Then who's in my room?" he demanded.

"No one's in your room," Mom said, sounding baffled.

Jonah whirled around and rushed up the stairs. He shoved open the door to his room, flipped on the light.

Nobody was there.

Jonah jerked the closet door open; he got down on his hands and knees and looked under the bed. He looked beside his desk, behind the door, all the places he'd ever used during hide-and-seek games when he was little.

"Jonah, honey, what are you doing?" Mom asked, appearing in his doorway.

"I thought I saw someone in my room," Jonah said. "When I was outside."

Mom peeked into the closet and under the bed.

"There's nobody here," she said. She took in a shaky breath. "Really, Jonah, if there'd been an intruder, we would have heard him. You know how those stairs creak."

Maybe whoever it was didn't use the stairs, Jonah thought. *Maybe he used a ladder at the back of the house. . . .*

Or maybe it was someone who could just appear and disappear at will, like Katherine's ghost.

Jonah didn't want to think about that. But he also didn't go to the back of the house to look for a ladder.

Dad walked into the room and laid his hands comfortingly on Mom's shoulders.

"Jonah, if you'd really thought there was an intruder,

you shouldn't have come rushing up here, putting yourself in danger. You should have called the police," he said.

Jonah sat down on his bed.

"It was just my imagination, I guess," he said sulkily. "If I'd called the police, they would have been mad."

"But you would have been safe," Dad said.

Mom sat down beside Jonah on the bed. She patted his shoulder.

"You've just had a hard day," she said. "It's been a little overwhelming for all of us."

"Yeah," Jonah said absently.

He was facing his desk, where he'd dumped the contents of his backpack after school, before they'd gone to see Mr. Reardon. Jonah hadn't been able to concentrate on homework—not enough to do it, and certainly not enough to put it all in a tidy stack—so he had a half-finished math sheet sliding into the paper giving instructions for his next language arts paragraph sliding into a sheet announcing the school's Halloween dance. But that wasn't what Jonah was looking at. On top of those papers, Jonah could see another one that was half–folded up, as if it had just been removed from an envelope.

He wasn't at the right angle to see everything written on the half-folded paper, but he could see a little bit: *"Bewa—"*

It was one of the mysterious letters he'd received, which he knew he'd left in the back of his top drawer, under his collection of state quarters.

Jonah remembered the tiny light hovering over his desk that he'd seen from outside.

"Are you *sure* you weren't in here a few moments ago, right before I got home?" Jonah asked his parents. Suddenly he *wanted* to believe that they'd been searching through his room, snooping around. It was better than any of the other possibilities.

"Jonah, we weren't," Dad said. "Neither one of us has been upstairs since before dinner."

Jonah could barely remember dinner. He and Katherine had rushed through the leftover chili so they could get to Chip's house.

Dad was peering at him with a concerned squint, worry lines ringing his eyes.

"Is something wrong?" Mom asked. "I mean, something we don't already know about?"

Was that the opening Jonah wanted? He did want to tell Mom and Dad about the letters—let them worry, so he wouldn't have to. But the tale of the letters now involved disappearing ghosts, and Katherine taking cell phone pictures of secret documents with Jonah's name on them, and *witnesses*, as if Jonah had been involved in some crime.

"Nothing's wrong," Jonah said. He yawned unconvincingly. "I'm just tired."

Mom and Dad were both still looking at him doubtfully, but it seemed like they were willing to play along.

"Maybe you should go to bed early," Mom said. Mom was big on the curative powers of sleep. Jonah was surprised she didn't add, "Everything will look better in the morning." Instead she said, "I'm glad you came back from Chip's. Was Katherine with you? I didn't see her. . . ." She looked around as if, having acted so worried about Jonah, she now had to show the same amount of concern about her daughter.

"She's still at Chip's," Jonah said.

By her face, Jonah thought he could practically see the calculation going on in Mom's head: *Goodness, there couldn't be anything romantic going on between those two, could there? She's only in sixth grade, but this is an older boy. . . .*

"She's got the cell phone with her, doesn't she?" Mom asked with studied casualness. "I think I'll give her a call, tell her to come on home. It's almost nine o'clock."

"I'll go get her," Jonah volunteered. He was still a little mad at his sister, but somehow he didn't want her walking home alone, along the dark street with all its eerie shadows.

Which was crazy, because *he* was the one who'd gotten the threatening letters.

Of course, she was the one who thought she'd seen a ghost. . . .

"Would you do that?" Mom asked. "Thanks."

Jonah waited until Mom and Dad were out of his room before he tucked the mysterious letter back in his drawer. Then he went outside. He was nearly back to Chip's house when he saw Katherine, slipping out of the Winstons' front door.

"Tomorrow," she was promising Chip. "We'll solve this. We will!"

Jonah waited until Chip had shut the door, and Katherine was stepping out onto the sidewalk. He hid behind a maple tree and then jumped out just as Katherine was passing by: "Boo!"

Katherine shrieked and then she giggled and then she pounded her fists against Jonah's chest.

"I *hate* you!" she screamed, laughing. "You're *terrible!*"

Jonah almost laughed too because it felt so good to treat everything like a joke, to pretend that he wasn't worried about anything. And, fortunately, Katherine's fists didn't hurt at all. She wasn't hitting very hard.

"Just for that, I'm not going to tell you what Chip and I found out," Katherine threatened.

"Good. I don't want to know anyhow," Jonah said. "Remember?"

"Okay, then, just for that, I'll tell you everything," Katherine corrected herself. "Chip and I called every name on the witnesses list."

Jonah thought about putting his hands over his ears and chanting, "I'm not listening! I'm not listening! La, la, la, la, la . . ." But he couldn't quite bring himself to do that.

"Two of the people just hung up on us," Katherine continued. "But I did get one guy to tell me that he worked as an air traffic controller. I was pretending that I was working on a career project for school, and I was supposed to call people at random and talk to them about their jobs. He was really friendly and wanted to talk and talk and talk—air traffic controllers must not get out much. But then I said, 'Did you ever witness anything unusual, like maybe thirteen years ago or so?' and he got really, really quiet, and then he said he had to go, he didn't have time to talk to me. That means something, don't you think?"

"No," Jonah said automatically, because he didn't want to believe that any of this meant anything.

"And then this other lady—Angela DuPre, her name was the first one on the list—she sounded perfectly normal when Chip first started talking to her. But then he laid everything on the line, about how he'd just found out that he was adopted, and he didn't know anything about

his birth parents, and he thought she might know something . . . and then she just totally freaked out. She started
hyperventilating, almost, and she said, 'I can't talk to you.
Don't call me ever again.' Weird, huh?"

It was all weird, Jonah thought, stepping in and out of
the shadows. He wanted to find normal explanations.

"Well, maybe—maybe she gave up a baby for adoption," he said. "Maybe it was, like, thirteen years ago, and
so she thought Chip might be her son and it was just all
too emotional for her. You know how some birth parents
want to reunite with their kids, and some never want to
have anything to do with them—they just want to pretend nothing ever happened. . . ." For the first time Jonah
actually kind of understood that viewpoint. Something
else struck him. "Hey, maybe she really is Chip's birth
mother. Or—or mine. Maybe that's what *witnesses* really
meant. Like, it's a code word or something."

"I don't think so," Katherine said.

"Why not?" Jonah challenged.

"It just didn't seem like that," Katherine said.

"Oh, right, you know all about these things," Jonah
scoffed. But his heart wasn't into it, because they'd reached
the point on the street where he could see into his bedroom windows—where he'd been standing when he'd seen
the intruder before. He couldn't help staring up at the

windows now, but they were blank and dark and empty.

He didn't tell Katherine about the intruder. He wouldn't tell her or Chip, and maybe he could forget about it himself.

"Jonah," Katherine said earnestly. "Chip and I really are going to figure all this out. And when we do, you'll thank us. You'll be so happy. You'll be—at peace."

They were at the front door now. Jonah put his hand on the doorknob. Home, which had looked like such a safe place before, was now just a place where he might see ghosts, where he had to worry about his secrets being pulled out for anyone to see, where he had to worry about Mom and Dad worrying about him. He already felt haunted.

"Katherine?" he said.

"What?" She turned to him eagerly.

"You don't know what you're talking about."

FIFTEEN

The next few days passed uneventfully. Jonah didn't get any more strange letters, and no one disturbed the letter he already had. He didn't see any evidence of ghosts or intruders.

Katherine and Chip kept insisting on giving him updates on their ongoing research project, no matter how many times Jonah said, "I don't care." He tried to ignore them. But he knew they wanted to call every single name on the survivors list now too.

"It'd be easier if Katherine had held the camera a little steadier," Chip told Jonah at the bus stop the third morning. "Look at this." He took a folded-up paper out of his pocket—the printout of the photos Chip had pieced together. He pointed at one spot, where there was a gap between the words. "Right here. She got the address and phone number of this person, but I don't know who to ask for when I call. And then, down here, right below that, she just got the name and the street address, not even a city name, so I can't look up their phone number online. It's frustrating."

"Huh," Jonah said, barely bothering to look at the paper. Then curiosity got the better of him. Since this was only Chip, not Katherine, he decided it was safe to ask at least one question.

"What are you even saying to these people when you call?"

"We ask who they are," Chip said. "What they survived. Why their names are on a list at the FBI."

"Do they know?" Jonah made sure he was looking away from Chip when he asked that, as if he was more concerned about watching for the bus than about hearing what Chip was saying.

"None of them know about the list. They've survived things like broken arms and chicken pox and minor car accidents and . . ." Chip gave Jonah a sidelong look, ". . . being adopted."

Jonah decided not to comment on that.

"They'll talk to you? Some stranger calling them out of the blue?" He wondered if everyone was as trusting as his parents.

"Usually not right away," Chip said. "Until I start talking about how I just found out I was adopted, and how I got these weird, kind of scary letters—and how my name's on that list of survivors too. Usually it's the letter part that gets them talking."

"They got the letters too," Jonah said. It wasn't a question. He could tell just from Chip's voice.

"Katherine already told you that, didn't she?" Chip asked. "Everyone we talked to got them."

Jonah didn't want to admit how hard he'd been working to tune out everything Katherine had tried to tell him. He looked around for his sister. She was in the center of the kids laughing and talking under the glow of the streetlight, but she wasn't joining in the laughter. She was peering anxiously at him and Chip.

"It's just been five or six people you've talked to, right?" Jonah said. "I think that's what Katherine said. That's not so many. Nothing to base any conclusions on. It's not a"—he tried to remember the proper term—"a statistically significant sample."

Wow—his math teacher would be really proud of him for remembering that.

"Jonah, it's seventeen people so far," Chip said.

Jonah remembered that Katherine hadn't been able to help Chip out the night before, because she'd had gymnastics practice. He felt a little guilty for not helping Chip himself.

"And," Chip continued, "every single 'survivor' I've talked to is adopted, just like us. They're all thirteen years old, or they'll turn thirteen within the next month. They all have fall birthdays. And all of them were about three months old when they were adopted."

Just like me, Jonah thought.

"What are they—clones?" he asked sarcastically. "Did you ask to check their DNA?"

"Jonah, eight of them are girls. Three are Asian. Two are black. They're not clones."

Jonah decided to stop making jokes.

"I haven't even told you the weirdest thing," Chip said. "Everybody lives here in Liston or in Upper Tyson or Clarksville." Upper Tyson and Clarksville were the two closest suburbs.

"So?" Jonah challenged. "How's that weird? Maybe this is just the territory for the FBI office I went to."

Chip shook his head.

"Most of the kids were adopted in other places, like me," Chip said. "But even the ones who used to live someplace else, they've all moved here. All within the past six months. That's twelve kids moving here, all since June."

Jonah had chills suddenly. Then he thought of something.

"Wait a minute—let me see that list again."

Chip pulled the papers back out of his pocket. Jonah yanked it out of his friend's hands and stabbed a finger at one line of print.

"See, this person you were asking me about before, that's an address in Ann Arbor, Michigan," he said triumphantly. "That's miles away, a whole different state. Maybe it's just a coincidence that Katherine only got the complete information on people who live close by. No, wait—here's somebody in Winnetka, Illinois. So, there are at least two people who live somewhere else—"

"Jonah, that's *me*, in Winnetka," Chip said. "I'm on the list twice, with my new address and my old one, both, just like I got two copies of each of those weird letters. . . ." His voice faltered. "Oh, I see. . . ."

"What?" Jonah thought of something new, too. "You think the FBI sent us the letters?"

"No . . . I don't know," Chip said distractedly. "But this person in Ann Arbor? It's a girl, and her name's Daniella McCarthy."

The only thing Jonah could see above the address, *103 Destin Court, Ann Arbor, Michigan*, was a little line, right above the *t* of *Court*. It might have been the loop of the *y* at the end of *McCarthy*. Or it might have been just a wrinkle in the paper, magnified and darkened by the camera.

"How do you figure that?" Jonah asked.

"I bet you anything it's the same girl as down here, the one at 1873 Robin's Egg Lane," Chip said. "And I bet there's a Robin's Egg Lane in Liston or Upper Tyson or Clarksville. That's the pattern on the entire list—old address, new address. . . . I bet if I call this Ann Arbor number, I'll get one of those messages, 'Doo-doo-doo . . . The number you are calling has been changed. The new number is . . .'" He'd made his voice robotic, just like a computerized phone message. Now he slipped back into his usual voice. "I'll prove it."

He pulled his cell phone out of his backpack and began dialing.

"Chip, do that later. The bus is coming," Jonah said, because he could see the headlights swinging around the corner.

"I'm just going to get a machine," Chip said. "Got anything to write with?"

Jonah fished a pen out of his own backpack. Chip held out his left palm.

"I'll repeat the number back to you. You write it on my hand," Chip said.

Chip was still talking when the phone clicked—Jonah was close enough to hear—and a decidedly noncomputerized voice said, "Hello?"

It sounded like a girl.

"Uh, hello," Chip said awkwardly. "Uh, Daniella?"

"Yes?" She sounded impatient.

"Um . . . you still live in Ann Arbor?"

"Where else would I live?"

"Uh, Liston, Ohio? Or maybe Upper Tyson or Clarks-ville, but that's not as likely—are you sure you aren't mov-ing or planning to move or in the process of—?"

"No," the girl said, in a tone that very clearly said, *that is such a stupid question.*

"Hey, you two going to school today?" the bus driver yelled.

Jonah realized that the bus had arrived and almost all the other kids had already climbed on. He jerked on Chip's arm, pulling him toward the bus.

"Um, sorry," Chip was saying into the phone. "I think I have some bad information. You really don't have another address on a Robin's Egg Lane in another city?"

Jonah couldn't hear what the girl said in reply, because they were stumbling up the steps. But a moment later, as they shoved their way down the aisle, Chip began plead-ing, "No, wait, don't hang up—are you adopted?"

"Great pickup line, dude," an eighth-grader muttered from his seat.

Chip lowered the phone from his ear.

"Let me guess—she hung up?" Jonah asked.

Chip nodded.

Both of them plopped into their seat as the bus pulled away from the curb.

"Wow—you really have a way with girls," Jonah wise-cracked.

Chip shook his head.

"I don't understand. This doesn't fit the pattern at all. And now she's all mad at me, just for asking—really, I did a much better job with all the other calls, or I had Katherine make them—"

"So just have Katherine call this Daniella back tonight and ask things the right way," Jonah said.

"You don't understand," Chip said. "I want to know every-thing *now*."

Chip slumped in the seat, staring at the cell phone as if it had betrayed him. He looked so miserable that Jonah felt obligated to cheer him up.

"Hey," Jonah said, jostling Chip's arm. "You and Katherine have been hanging out together a lot. Do you still have a crush on her?"

It was strange, how talking about Chip's liking Katherine had become the *safe* topic.

"I can't think about crushes and girls and all that right now," Chip mumbled. "Not when I don't even know who I am."

"You're Chip Winston," Jonah said firmly. He felt like he was replaying the conversation he'd had with Katherine the night he'd gotten the second letter. Except he was taking the Katherine role.

Chip didn't answer right away. Jonah wondered if he'd even heard him. Then, so softly that Jonah had to lean in to hear him, Chip whispered, "Can I tell you something? Even before I found out I was adopted, even before I knew Mom and Dad weren't really my parents—biological parents, I mean—I always felt like there was something wrong with me. Something different. Like I wasn't who I was supposed to be. Like I never belonged. Not here. Not back in Winnetka. Not anywhere."

Jonah leaned away and squinted at Chip in distress. Kids weren't supposed to say stuff like that to other kids. What if somebody else heard him? Jonah looked around. Marcus Gladstone was drumming his fingers on the seat in front of him. Owen Rogers was doing his math homework, muttering, "Come on, come on, multiply both sides by twelve . . . carry the four. . . ." Queen Jackson was telling Nila Holcomb, "That boy is just bad news." Jonah was pretty sure she wasn't talking about him or Chip.

Chip hadn't even looked up. He was still talking, his eyes trained on the seat back in front of him.

"—And it seems like, this whole adoption thing, maybe

that's my answer. Maybe once I find out everything and get an explanation, then I'll *know*—"

Jonah shoved his shoulder against Chip's shoulder.

"Hey," he interrupted harshly. "Stop that." He tried to remember the argument Katherine had used on him. "Weren't you paying attention in that guidance assembly the other day? All teenagers wonder who they are. It's part of growing up."

Jonah couldn't believe he'd been forced to use such a goopy line. Now he was as embarrassed for himself as he was for Chip. He hoped no one else had heard *him*.

"I think this is different," Chip said quietly. He paused, as if to give Jonah a chance to say, "I know what you mean." Or to admit, "You're totally right. I've felt the same way. And not just since I turned thirteen." When Jonah didn't say anything, Chip went on. "And don't you see? This is *big*. All these kids, and the FBI, and—and *ghosts* . . ."

"But it doesn't make any sense," Jonah said.

"I was working on a theory," Chip said. He held up his cell phone. "Until our friend Daniella messed everything up."

"So what was the theory?"

Before Chip could answer, the phone in his hand began to ring, blaring a Fall Out Boy tune. Quickly, Chip flipped it open and looked at the number.

"Seven-three-four area code . . . is that—" He raised the phone to his ear. "Daniella?"

"Who are you?" Daniella was evidently shouting, because this time Jonah didn't even have to lean close to hear every word. "How did you know?"

Chip moved the phone away from his head, gave it a baffled look, then placed it back against his ear.

"I—what are you talking about?" he asked.

"We *are* moving!" Daniella screamed. Her voice blared from the phone. "This is so awful! My life is over!"

"I thought you said you weren't," Chip said cautiously.

"I didn't know!" From the way her voice sounded, Jonah suspected that Daniella was about to cry. "My dad made this big 'family announcement' at breakfast—he's taking a job transfer, and that little 'getaway' my parents were on was actually a house-hunting trip! They're going to make an offer on a house today. What are you—the realtor's kid?"

"Er, no. Actually—"

Daniella didn't seem to hear him.

"That wasn't funny at all, if that's your idea of a prank," she fumed. "Or, were you trying to talk me into thinking I was going to like the house? I won't. My parents say it's 'wonderful.'" She made *wonderful* sound like something evil. "I bet it's a pit!"

"Hold on," Jonah said, struggling to catch up with all of Daniella's fury-by-phone. "Did she say her parents are making an offer on the house *today*? They don't own it already?"

Chip squinted in puzzlement.

"You're talking about the house on Robin's Egg Lane, right?" Chip said into the phone. He struggled to pull out the survivors list from his pocket, unfold it, and find the right number. "Um—1873 Robin's Egg Lane? In"—he bit his lip, obviously making a guess—"Liston, Ohio?"

"Yes, yes, that's what you asked me about. Mom and Dad saw it yesterday and just 'fell in love with it.'" She twisted the words bitterly, so it sounded like they'd fallen into the deep fiery pits of Hades.

Jonah leaned in close and spoke into the phone: "You say they just saw the house yesterday? For the very first time?"

"Yes . . . ," Daniella moaned. "Yesterday, for the first time. And, just like that, they're going to try to buy it today. I think they're having a midlife crisis. They're insane. Why do they have to ruin my life?" Now Jonah was certain: she was crying. Her words kept dissolving into wails. "I hate Ohio! I'm going to be miserable there! I—I—" She sniffled. "I can't talk anymore. I'm too upset."

The next thing Jonah heard was a dial tone.

Chip slowly lowered the phone from his ear.

"She'll call back," he said confidently. "She didn't give me a chance to answer any of her questions."

"But she answered ours," Jonah said.

"Not that she let us ask much!" Chip snorted. "I still need to know if she's adopted, and if she got the same kind of letters we got, and if she knows what we all 'survived,' and . . ." Chip seemed to be working from some sort of mental checklist.

"Chip, don't you get it? Those questions don't matter right now." Jonah eased the survivors list out of Chip's hand and held it up. "I got this list three days ago, with Daniella McCarthy's address on Robin's Egg Lane. Her parents didn't even see the house until yesterday. They haven't made an offer on it yet, but they're going to today. So"—he shook the list in Chip's face—"how did the FBI know the future?"

"They couldn't have," Chip said.

Seconds passed while both of them stared hard at the list, the three-day-old list from the FBI that contained information no one should have been able to know until today. Jonah knew that they were almost at school, that the bus around them was filled with kids laughing and flirting and teasing and griping and even—here and there—

singing. But Jonah couldn't focus on anything except the survivors list. That and Chip's voice, saying slowly, "Unless . . ."

"Unless what?" Jonah asked.

"Unless they're the ones making her move."

SIXTEEN

"That's ridiculous," Jonah said. "Impossible."

"Why?" Chip asked.

Jonah barely stopped himself from giving an answer that would have sounded like his dad: "Because the government is set up to serve the people. Not to ruin kids' lives by making them move." Instead he mumbled, "Why would they care where Daniella McCarthy lives? How could it matter to them? And to direct her family to that exact house—"

"Maybe one of Daniella's parents is a top-secret scientist," Chip said, "and some enemy is about to drop a bomb on their house, and so the FBI is moving them for their own safety. . . ."

Jonah frowned at Chip and rolled his eyes.

"It's Daniella's name on the list," Jonah said. "Not her parents'."

"Maybe that's just some sort of code," Chip argued.

"What about all the other thirteen-year-olds on the list? Are all of our names some kind of code?" Jonah asked. "*My* parents aren't top-secret scientists, I can tell you that. And nobody's ever tried to make us move." Still, Jonah felt a knot of anxiety in his stomach at the thought of moving. He'd lived his whole life in the same house— well, his whole life since he'd been adopted. "My mom would never agree to leave our house, not even if the president himself begged her to," he said. "She's spent too much time babying that rhododendron bush in our backyard. And her roses and her grapevines and every- thing else . . ."

Jonah had never cared that much about the rhododen- dron bush; he'd always thought Mom made way too much of a fuss about "those gorgeous blooms" and "Do you think they're a little smaller than usual? Should I test the soil acidity again?" But now he pictured Mom clutching the trunk of the bush while some official-looking government types tried to pull her away: them arguing, "But you have to go!" while she countered, "I'll never leave! Never!"

The image was strangely comforting.

"Hey!"

Jonah looked up to see the bus driver in the aisle in front of them. He was glowering.

"Let me explain something to you two," he growled. "I pull up to your bus stop, you get on the bus. I pull up to your school, you get off. It's not that complicated."

Jonah realized that they were at school now; he and Chip were the only kids still on the bus.

"Oh, sorry!" he said, jumping up, grabbing his backpack.

"Maybe you want to go to the elementary school instead?" the bus driver asked. He seemed amused now. "That's my next run. This is the day when all the little kids stay on the bus extra-long, to learn bus safety. Maybe you need that, just to learn to get on and off?"

"No, no, that's okay," Chip mumbled, scrambling up behind Jonah.

The bus driver stepped back between two of the seats to let them past him in the aisle. He was laughing at them.

"What a jerk," Jonah muttered, as soon as they were out on the sidewalk. Other kids from other buses streamed past them, into the school. He tried to blend into the crowd. At least no one else had been on the bus to hear the driver making fun of them.

Chip grabbed Jonah's arm.

"After school I'm going to call Daniella back," Chip said. "Maybe she'll have calmed down by then. And I want to call back the other kids on the list, to ask why they moved. You'll help now, won't you? Remember what you promised me? 'I'll do everything I can to help you.'"

Chip's imitation of Jonah's voice was frighteningly accurate.

I didn't know what I was promising, Jonah wanted to argue. *That was last week. I thought I'd just have to quote from* What to Tell Your Adopted and Foster Children. *Not solve mysteries. Not see ghosts. Not call strangers. Not figure out the FBI. Not . . . worry about my own past.*

Chip's blue eyes were pleading and desperate.

"Katherine's all right and everything, but she's too . . . cheerful about all of this," Chip said. "She's thinks it's fun."

What's wrong with fun? Jonah wanted to ask. But he knew exactly what Chip meant.

"All right," Jonah said reluctantly. "After school."

The day dragged. Jonah couldn't concentrate on any of his classes. More than once, his teachers noticed and said, "Jonah? Are you with us?" or "Jonah? Didn't you hear me the first *five* times I asked everyone to open their books?"

On the bus ride home, Jonah made sure he and Chip didn't get too distracted. They were the first ones off the bus when it reached their stop.

Katherine bounced up eagerly behind them.

"How many names do you want to call today?" she

asked. "I don't have gymnastics tonight, and I did all my homework in study center, so I am ready to start dialing!"

Chip and Jonah exchanged glances.

"Well, see, I've got to get the mail first," Chip said weakly. "And then . . ."

"No problem. I can wait," Katherine said, grinning.

She followed the boys to the Winstons' brick mailbox. Chip took his time about reaching in, drawing out the stacks of letters and magazines and junk mail. Jonah felt like telling him, *Look, if you think Katherine is going to get bored and leave, forget it. Once she's into something, she never gives up.*

Chip was so completely into his act, trying to get rid of Katherine, that he just stood there, staring at the stack of letters.

Maybe it wasn't an act.

"Chip?" Jonah asked cautiously. "Is something wrong?"

Jonah remembered that lists and ghosts and the FBI weren't all they had to worry about. He remembered that letters had been the first signs of strangeness.

"Chip?" Jonah repeated.

Chip held up a letter.

"It's addressed to me, and there's no return address," he said. "But it's not like the others."

He was right. This letter was in a smaller envelope,

the kind used for invitations. And Chip's address wasn't typed but written—in firm grown-up handwriting, like a teacher's.

"Open it!" Katherine said excitedly. "Let's see what this one says!"

Jonah turned to glare at his sister—what was wrong with her? Wasn't she scared at all? How could she act so thrilled when he felt almost paralyzed with dread?

Katherine missed his glare because she was snatching the envelope out of Chip's hand, ripping the letter open.

"Whoa," she breathed.

"What is it?" Jonah asked. He discovered he wasn't completely paralyzed. He could crane his neck and peer over Katherine's shoulder.

The letter was on a piece of generic white paper. Unfolded, it said:

You contacted me at 8:35 p.m. on Monday, October 2. I was not at liberty to discuss anything with you over the phone. If you call back, I will deny that I sent this letter. I will refuse to tell you anything more. But if it is safe, I will meet you in conference room B at the Liston Public Library at 3:00 p.m. on Saturday, October 7. Then we can talk.

Do not attempt to contact me otherwise. This is the only way.

There was no signature.

SEVENTEEN

"Angela DuPre," Katherine said.

"Wh-what?" Jonah stammered.

"That's who this is from," Katherine said confidently, waving the letter in Jonah's face. "Remember, Chip, she was the only one from the witnesses list who seemed kind of, I don't know, regretful about hanging up on us. Is *regretful* a word?"

Jonah didn't care about words right now.

"Well, it could have been—what was that other woman's name?—Monique Waters?" Chip suggested.

"Oh, no," Katherine said. "That woman *loved* hanging up on us. She was cold."

"And the air traffic controller talked to you, not me," Chip said, "so he wouldn't send me a letter—"

"And this is definitely a woman's handwriting. Definitely," Katherine said.

Jonah was getting annoyed with their little junior detective routine.

"So are you going?" he asked. "On Saturday?"

Chip and Katherine both stopped talking. Both of them froze with their mouths hanging open. It wasn't a good look for either of them.

Then Katherine laughed.

"Of course," she said. "We have to!"

"This is a complete stranger," Jonah said. "She won't even sign her name. She won't talk to you on the telephone. She sounds crazy. This is how people end up getting kidnapped."

"But she's got information," Chip said. "She might know who I am."

Chip sounded so plaintive, Jonah couldn't argue anymore.

"If you're going to kidnap someone, you wouldn't ask to meet at the library," Katherine said. "That conference room B—that's where we used to have Brownie meetings when I was a little kid. It's, like, glass on three sides. And you have to walk through the whole library to get to it. It's safe."

Jonah shrugged. He felt strangely dizzy, just like he had that time in Florida when he'd gotten caught in a riptide, and the flimsy little flutter kick he'd learned at the

Liston Pool had been no match for the forces carrying him out to sea.

Jonah's dad had jumped in and saved him that time.

He can't save me now, Jonah thought despairingly. *We can't tell Mom and Dad anything about this. Can't tell them we're meeting a stranger. Can't tell them we've been calling strangers. Can't tell them we took pictures of a secret file . . .*

"Besides," Katherine was saying. "There'll be three of us together, and no one adult could kidnap three kids."

"How can you be so sure that she won't bring anybody with her?" Jonah asked, at the same time that Chip said, "What if seeing all three of us scares her off? She sounds a little paranoid—I think it has to be just me."

"Well, we're all going," Katherine said. "There's no question about that!"

They didn't get a chance to call any of the kids on the survivors list that afternoon—or the next—because they were so busy debating their strategy for meeting with Angela DuPre (if that was really who'd written the letter). Saturday morning, Jonah had a soccer game and Katherine had a piano lesson, but by two o'clock they were both in Chip's driveway, on their bikes, waiting. Jonah focused on balancing carefully, lifting his toes from the concrete on first the left side, then the right. He could straddle the bike for seconds at a time without touching the ground.

As long as he concentrated on that little game, he didn't have to think about the fact that he and Katherine and Chip were about to do something incredibly stupid and probably dangerous as well.

"You didn't really leave a note, did you?" Katherine asked, breaking Jonah's concentration and forcing him to slam his right foot down to the ground to keep from falling.

"I did," Jonah said.

Katherine rolled her eyes.

The note was Jonah's attempt at caution. They'd told Mom and Dad only that they were riding their bikes to the library. But in his desk drawer, Jonah had left a detailed note—a letter, really—explaining that they were meeting a woman named Angela DuPre (or possibly Monique Waters) and if for some reason they didn't come back, someone should track her down. All the information about possible kidnappers would be on Chip Winston's computer.

Katherine and Chip thought he was crazy for being so careful.

Katherine sighed, blowing the air out in a way that ruffled the hair on her forehead.

"Wish Mom could have driven us," she said. "Nobody rides bikes anymore."

"I do," Jonah said.

"Girls, I mean," Katherine said. "All my friends think bikes are babyish. No one had better see me."

She looked around anxiously. The street was deserted.

Riding bikes versus being driven had caused a huge debate. Chip thought if they had a parent drive them, they'd have to explain why they had to be at the library exactly at three o'clock, rather than after their moms got through at the grocery store, or before their dads started watching the football game. And Jonah thought that if they had to make a quick getaway, it'd be ridiculous to stand there in the library lobby calling a parent, "Uh, yeah, I'm ready to be picked up. Do you mind not waiting until halftime? There's kind of a murderous psychopath chasing me. . . ."

"What do you really think is going to happen?" Katherine asked.

Jonah shrugged. She'd been asking him that question for two days. And he'd never been able to explain that, exactly, even to himself. He didn't truly believe that they were about to face a murderous psychopath. He just had a horrible feeling in the pit of his stomach that wouldn't go away.

The garage door of Chip's house began rising, revealing Chip and his bike. Chip was grinning.

"Time for some answers!" he proclaimed. Jonah thought

maybe Chip was trying to sound like the donkey from
Shrek—carefree, glib, and full of wisecracks even in the face
of danger. But it wasn't a very good imitation, because his
voice cracked.

"First we've got to ride all the way over there," Katherine
complained. "What is it—two miles? Three?"

"We don't have to go," Jonah said.

"Of course we do," Chip said, pushing off and sailing
out into the street.

Jonah let Katherine follow Chip, and then he sighed
and brought up the rear. It was weird how responsible he
felt for the other two: plaintive, pitiful, confused Chip;
naïve, gung-ho, enthusiastic Katherine. He and Chip were
both equally tall and gangly—it wasn't like Jonah had any
extra muscles for fighting off attackers.

There's strength in numbers, he told himself, peddling hard
to catch up.

They passed the BP station where the high-school
band boosters were having a car-wash fund-raiser; the
grocery store where Mom was right now buying pea-
nut butter and milk and bread, like it was any Saturday
afternoon; the neighborhood that, according to a quick
Google search they'd done, contained the Robin's Egg
Lane where Daniella McCarthy's family would soon be
moving. They got to the library by two thirty.

Chip was looking at his watch before he even slipped off his bike.

"I've still got to wait another half hour?" he said. "I thought the ride would take longer than that."

"This will give us a chance to case the joint," Katherine said. Jonah *knew* she'd gotten that line from a movie. "And enough time to man our stations."

Deciding how many of them should be in conference room B at three o'clock had sparked their longest and bitterest debate. They'd eventually reached a compromise: Chip would be the only one actually in the conference room. But he'd secretly have his cell phone set on speaker phone in his lap, and he'd call Katherine, who'd be hiding out in the magazine section. She'd hold the cell phone up to both her ear and a walkie-talkie, broadcasting to the other walkie-talkie in Jonah's hand. Jonah would be in the nonfiction section, near the conference room. He'd be pretending to read, facing away from the conference room, but he'd secretly have a mirror hidden in his book, directed over his shoulder, so he could see what was happening to Chip every single minute. The walkie-talkie– phone combo would let him hear everything that was going on in the conference room. So at the first hint of danger, he'd be able to storm in and save Chip.

They'd planned everything. None of them, even once,

had said, "This is ridiculous! Walkie-talkies? Mirrors hidden in books? We'll look like fools!" Jonah thought maybe that was proof that, underneath it all, the other two were every bit as scared as he was.

They leaned their bikes against the bike rack and tiptoed into the library. They peeked into conference room B—no one was there—and tested out the cell phone–walkie-talkie setup.

"Spy One to Spy Two," Katherine said, giggling into the walkie-talkie. "Over."

Jonah switched the walkie-talkie function to SEND.

"Katherine, it works, but, so help me, you've got to remember—you're not supposed to do any of the talking!"

At two fifty-five, Jonah flipped the hood of his sweatshirt up so it covered the walkie-talkie pressed against his ear. He pulled a book off a nonfiction shelf at random—it was something about tax codes. He positioned Katherine's makeup mirror in the book, angled it just so . . . yep, there was Chip's face, anxious and pale on the other side of the conference room's glass wall. Jonah moved the mirror up and down and side to side, scanning the whole room. He switched the walkie-talkie to SEND again.

"Katherine, tell Chip to stop fiddling with the cell phone," he whispered urgently. "He'll give us away."

Seconds later, in the mirror, Chip jerked upright. He

put his hands flat on the conference room table, on top of the printouts of the survivors and witnesses lists he'd brought from home. He raised an eyebrow at Jonah. Over his shoulder, Jonah gave him the thumbs-up signal.

Katherine's giggle sounded in Jonah's ear again.

"Remember your theory about this woman actually being Chip's birth mother?" she whispered. "You can cross that one off your list!"

Jonah started to say, "Why?" but then he remembered that *he* needed to be silent too. Over the walkie-talkie, he heard a static-y version of Chip's voice: "Oh, hello. Are you the person who reserved this conference room for three o'clock? The one who's willing to talk?"

Frantically, Jonah angled the mirror, turning his tax code book almost sideways. There. A woman, walking into the conference room. Oh. A tall, statuesque, well-dressed *black* woman. Very dark-skinned—definitely not Chip's birth mother.

"Chip Winston?" the woman was saying.

"Yes," Chip said cautiously. "And you are—?"

The woman stopped in the conference room doorway and looked back over her shoulder. Her eyes seemed to meet Jonah's in the mirror. She laughed.

"Before we begin, I'll have to ask you to turn that cell phone off," she said. "And tell your friends to turn off the walkie-talkies. I appreciate their ingenuity, but they might as well come on in and listen in person."

"I—I don't know what you're talking about," Chip stammered.

"You're not a very good liar, are you?" the woman said. "I'll have to remember that. I'm talking about the girl in the magazine section, in the purple shirt, and the boy in the tax section, reading *Your Guide to the IRS* upside down."

Jonah blushed. He started to turn the book around, then realized that that made him look even more guilty. Out of the corner of his eye, he saw Katherine standing up, rushing toward the conference room. He waved his arms at her, trying to send a telepathic message, *No, no, go back! Pretend you've got nothing to do with me or Chip! Act normal! Don't give anything away!*

Katherine ignored him. She reached the door into the conference room and began shaking the woman's hand.

"Katherine Skidmore," she introduced herself. "Nice to meet you. Thanks for letting me join you."

Katherine made it sound like they were going to be sitting around eating sugar cookies and drinking lemonade.

"Come on, Jonah," Katherine said. "She's got us figured out."

Jonah whirled around.

"But I don't have to go in there, do I?" he muttered

through gritted teeth. "I can stay out here if I want to. So I can run for help if anything happens."

Jonah was surprised to see that the woman's dark eyes were sympathetic.

"You're the one I want guarding the door, then," she said. "Watching out for trouble. You can watch from the outside or watch from the inside. I don't care."

She looked around, scanning the rows of bookshelves around them. No one was in sight.

"I'm Angela DuPre," the woman said, holding out her hand to Jonah. "You can call me Angela."

Hesitantly, Jonah moved forward to shake her hand. He stepped in through the glass door behind Katherine and Angela, and pulled the door shut. But he didn't sit down at the table when the others did. He stayed by the door. Angela nodded respectfully at him, as if she approved of that choice.

"A little advice," Angela said, a hint of laughter in her voice. "The next time you do a stake-out, don't enter the building together." It was Jonah she looked at now. "I got here at two. I've been watching the three of you for the past half hour."

Jonah's face burned.

"I guess the walkie-talkies were a stupid idea," he mumbled.

"Oh, it was creative," Angela said. "I would have left you to your spy games if it weren't for the range on those things—I didn't want our conversation broadcast to every trucker passing by on the highway. Or . . . others who might want to listen."

She no longer sounded amused. Her eyes looked haunted.

Katherine was glaring at Angela.

"Oh, that's right," Katherine said, almost in the same snarly cat-fight voice she used when she was mad at her friends. "You're afraid to even talk on the phone."

"I have my reasons," Angela said softly, and somehow that shut Katherine up.

"But it's safe to talk now?" Chip asked eagerly, leaning forward. "You can give us answers?"

Angela gave another cautious look around, through the glass walls into the library, then through the windows into the parking lot. Jonah realized for the first time that Angela had taken the one seat in the room that backed up to a solid brick wall. Even if Jonah weren't guarding the door, she'd made sure that nobody could sneak up on her.

"You're curious about your adoption, right?" Angela said. "What makes you think that I know anything about it?"

Quickly, Chip explained about the list of survivors and the list of witnesses, shoving the papers over to her so she could look for herself.

"See, Jonah's name is on the list of survivors too," Katherine chimed in. "Mine isn't. I'm not adopted, but I'm the one who took the pictures."

Oh, good for you! Braggart! Jonah thought. Angela glanced at him just then, and Jonah could swear she knew what he was thinking. She smiled at him.

"I can tell you what I witnessed thirteen years ago," she said. "Even though I'm not supposed to discuss it with anyone. You'll probably think I'm crazy, anyhow."

Chip was leaning so far forward now that Jonah was afraid he might fall out of his chair.

"You know where I came from?" Chip asked. "Where *we* came from?"

Angela was shaking her head, frowning ruefully.

"Not where, exactly," she said apologetically. "But I think I might have a pretty good guess about when."

EIGHTEEN

"When?" Chip repeated numbly.

Jonah was thinking that maybe English wasn't his native language, after all. Maybe he'd spent his first few months of life hearing some other language, and maybe that was why he couldn't make Angela's words make sense in his head.

Katherine started laughing.

"Oh, thanks," she said sarcastically. "That makes everything as clear as mud." She flipped her hair over her shoulder. "We already know the 'when.' Chip and Jonah were both adopted thirteen years ago."

"Twelve years, ten months and, uh, four days, to be exact," Chip said.

Angela narrowed her eyes, looking at Katherine.

"Perhaps you'd like to hear my story before you dismiss it?" Angela asked.

"Please," Jonah said, and he was proud of himself, that he'd managed to say that much when he was feeling so jangly and strange.

Angela looked down at the table, and it occurred to Jonah that maybe she was nervous too. Nervous, talking to a couple of kids? That didn't make sense either.

"Thirteen years ago," Angela began softly, "I worked exactly one day at Sky Trails Airlines."

Katherine opened her mouth, and Jonah could tell she was about to say something snarky and mean, like, "Wow—did you get fired after one day? Or were you just too lazy to go back for day two?"

Jonah glared at his sister; he pressed his thumb and forefinger together and drew them across his lips, the universal sign for *Shut up!* He hoped the full force of his glare plus the gesture would let her know, *If you say one more nasty thing, I will throw you out. And Chip and I won't tell you a single word that Angela says, so you won't know a thing. . . .*

Katherine coughed.

"Um—Sky Trails?" she said weakly.

"It's an old airline—probably none of you have heard of it, because it went out of business about ten years ago," Angela said. "It went bankrupt, didn't pay any of its creditors. But I still get a disability check from Sky Trails, every single month."

Disability? Jonah thought. That was for people who couldn't work anymore because they were too sick or, well, disabled. Angela looked as if she could run a marathon—even in those funky high heels she was wearing. And, anyhow, Jonah had had some vague notion that disability checks came from the government, not private businesses.

Angela was looking around—from Katherine to Jonah to Chip—as if she expected one of them to ask another question. No one said anything. Angela sighed.

"That one day at Sky Trails changed my life," she said. "What I saw—well, you won't believe me, and nobody else will back up my story. But I know what I saw. I'm not crazy!"

Oh, Jonah thought. *Can people maybe get disability checks for being crazy, too?*

Angela shrugged.

"I can tell by your eyes you're already starting to doubt me," she said in a voice that was strangely choked. Jonah wondered: why would it matter to Angela whether three kids believed her?

"But," Angela continued, "I'm going to tell you this anyway. I think I have to."

"Okay," Chip said.

Angela clasped her hands together on the table, seeming to steel herself for the story ahead.

"During my one day as a gate agent at Sky Trails, an unidentified plane arrived at the airport," Angela said. "It was an unscheduled landing, completely unexpected. Depending on who you believe, either the radar was out of order briefly while it was landing—or it just appeared. Out of nowhere."

Jonah saw Katherine stiffen.

"I was evidently the only person who saw it appear," Angela said. "The only person who was looking."

"Did it disappear, too?" Katherine asked in a small voice.

Angela shot her a surprised look.

"I wasn't planning to get to that part until later," Angela said. "But . . . yes."

"I saw something like that happen once too," Katherine admitted. "Not a whole plane appearing and disappearing, but a person. A man."

"So you know what it's like," Angela said slowly. "Knowing exactly what you saw, but thinking that it couldn't possibly have happened like that. Second-guessing yourself. Having other people make fun of you because you won't say, 'Oh, I must have made a mistake.'"

"Exactly," Katherine said, nodding eagerly.

Any second now, they'd be throwing themselves into hugs, sobbing onto each other's shoulders, proclaiming, "Nobody understands me but you!"

"Can we get back to the story?" Chip interrupted. "That plane—was I on it? Was Jonah? Did it crash—is that why we're listed as survivors? I'll want to look at the records and find out where it came from, maybe talk to the pilot. . . ."

Angela snorted.

"It didn't crash," she said. "But good luck finding any records. Or the pilot."

"But—but—" Chip sputtered.

Angela's look was sympathetic again.

"I'm willing to bet that you two were on that plane," she said. "There were lots of babies. And if I was listed as a witness and you were listed as survivors—that's the only thing I've ever witnessed where government agents got involved like that."

"But—*why* were government agents involved?" Jonah asked. "A plane landed, it didn't crash—big deal."

Somehow, he could gloss over the whole appearing/disappearing part of the story, just as he'd glossed over it when Katherine was telling about the vanishing man in Mr. Reardon's office. He believed in ignoring unpleasant facts, in hopes that they'd go away.

"An *unauthorized* plane landed," Angela corrected him. "That's supposed to set off an alert for the entire airport. There's a whole protocol to be followed in those situations that I, being new, forgot about. But when I heard the first baby crying . . ."

Me? Jonah thought. *Was I crying?*

"Wasn't the baby with its parents?" Chip asked. "Or some adult?"

Angela looked him straight in the eye.

"The plane was full of babies. Thirty-six of them," she said. "But there wasn't a single adult aboard."

Chip laughed, a bitter sound in the sudden silence.

"What—babies were flying the plane? You expect me to believe that? 'Goo-goo, gaa-gaa, air traffic control, this is baby plane one, over,'" he mocked. "It sounds like something out of a diaper commercial."

Angela fixed him with a steely look.

"The FBI's theory was that there *had* been a pilot, a co-pilot, a whole flight crew, but they escaped somehow. Even though there were security cameras at the gate, and none of them showed anyone leaving the plane before I stepped on."

"So maybe there was a secret door somewhere, out of the camera's view," Jonah said. "Or maybe it was an experimental high-tech plane that worked on autopilot." He was still looking for realistic explanations. But if "experimental high-tech . . . autopilot" was the best he could do, he was really getting desperate.

"*You* think the pilot and flight crew just vanished into thin air," Katherine said, her voice ringing with confidence.

"Possibly," Angela said. "Or . . ."

She stopped. That one word hung in midair, tantalizingly.

"Or?" Jonah prompted.

Angela shook her head.

"I'll work up to that one," she said dryly. "Chip will just start laughing at me again."

"I'm sorry," Chip said, though he didn't really sound like he meant it. "You're making this all *Twilight Zone*-ish, but it just seems like—well, what Mr. Reardon told Jonah and Katherine sounds about right. There was some sort of baby-smuggling ring, and they were forced to land—maybe the police were shooting them down; maybe they just ran out of gas or oil or whatever planes use. But anyhow, the people ran away and left the babies behind, because they didn't want to get caught. So, really, as long as the FBI or INS or whoever looked at the plane, if they looked at, I don't know, the instruction book in the cockpit, to see what language it was written in—then there should have been lots of clues about where we came from. And surely they have all that in their records and—"

"You forgot what I said," Angela said in a steely voice. "The plane disappeared."

"Maybe it didn't disappear exactly," Chip said. "Maybe they just towed it away and you thought—er . . ."

His voice trailed off because both Angela and Katherine were glaring at him, full force.

"I told you you wouldn't believe me," Angela said, and she sounded so sad that Jonah felt guilty on Chip's behalf. Jonah wasn't sure what to make of Angela's story either, but he wasn't going to tell her that.

"Shall I continue?" Angela asked.

Meekly, all three kids nodded.

"Before I knew what was going on, there were FBI agents there and police and airport officials and airlines officials and all sorts of other officials I couldn't even identify," Angela said. "They were treating the whole airplane like a crime scene. A mystery to solve. But, you know, there were all those babies, and when one started crying, they all started crying. And you could just tell, it was driving those official types crazy. So they organized this baby brigade, and we had all these people carrying the babies off the plane—we were supposed to pay close attention to which seat each baby had come from, in case that was important. We didn't have carriers or strollers or anything like that, so we just closed off the entire gate area and lined the babies up on the floor. We were just lucky none of them was old enough to be crawling yet. . . ."

Jonah had been to the airport a couple of times: once when he was in third grade, and his Cub Scout troop had taken a field trip to learn about planes, and once when his family had gone to Disney World, and Dad hadn't wanted to drive. Jonah could just imagine the chaos of thirty-six babies being taken off a plane at once. But surely it would have been chaos—surely lots of people would have seen.

Angela was still talking.

"The moment we had all the babies off the plane—and all the agents and officials and airline personnel were off the plane too, because they were trying to get the babies sorted out—at that moment, I looked back. And I could see the plane, just like normal, just like I could see the carpet under my feet or the rubber lining around the door or my hand in front of my own face. It was there! And then it was gone, there was nothing there except air, and I could see straight out to the runway lights and the satellite dishes and the highway. . . ."

Even now, thirteen years later, Angela's voice was full of wonderment. It was like she was still amazed, still stunned.

"And, once again, you were the only one to see this?"

Chip asked, making no effort to keep the skepticism out of his voice.

Angela turned her head sharply.

"No," she said. "Monique saw the plane disappear—Monique Waters, my boss. But later, when Monique saw how things were going, she denied it all. *She* was the one who filled out the disability papers, saying I was delusional and prone to hallucinations and unfit to work at Sky Trails."

"How do you know she saw it disappear?" Chip asked.

"Because she screamed out, 'Holy crap! Where'd that plane go?'" Angela said, grinning slightly.

Jonah was trying to absorb this. He sort of wanted to believe Angela—he was sure that *she* believed what she was telling them. But it was too incredible.

"What about the other people?" Katherine began. "Didn't any of them—?"

"It was dark out," Angela said. "We were all carrying babies—you try to take care of thirty-six infants and still manage to think clearly! I think some of the other people might have seen the plane vanish, but then this one guy, James Reardon—"

"The one we talked to," Katherine interrupted.

Angela nodded.

"He started running around, taking charge, telling

people, 'All right, my agency has the plane towed away now; we'll handle it from here. We'll advise you if we discover anything that's relevant to your department. Thanks for your help.' And later I kind of wondered, maybe some of those people had seen weird things like that before and had decided to pretend that they didn't exist. To be able to keep their jobs. It was close to Christmastime; they were happy to be sent home—of course none of them had seen the plane appear from nowhere and vanish into nothing, both, so they could believe the official story more easily. . . ."

"Nobody went to the news media?" Chip asked. "Nobody put it out on the Internet? Not that the plane vanished, even, but just that there was this mysterious bunch of babies . . . Didn't we make CNN?"

His voice sounded mocking, but when Jonah glanced his way, Chip's face was deadly serious.

Angela shrugged.

"The Internet wasn't the big deal it is today," she said. "And we weren't supposed to contact any newspapers or TV stations. James Reardon wanted us all to sign confidentiality statements. But I . . . refused."

"Is that why you lost your job?" Jonah asked.

"Pretty much," Angela said. "Monique told me not to come back until I was ready to sign. I was never ready. I did talk to a newspaper reporter, I did call a TV station—but when everyone else said I was crazy, what good did it do?" She held her hands out, a gesture of helplessness.

Jonah tried to imagine being like Angela, standing up for the truth. He didn't think he could be so brave.

"Why did it matter so much to you?" Chip asked.

"I know what I saw," Angela said fiercely. "I trust my own eyes. And I wasn't going to lie because—because I thought it might be important. I thought the babies might be important. I thought we should really investigate, not just pretend nothing ever happened."

"So *you've* investigated, haven't you?" Katherine said, jumping ahead. Her eyes were glowing, like she'd found a new hero.

"That's one way of looking at it," Angela agreed. "The more common view would be that I've become a total crackpot, totally obsessed. My own family thinks I'm crazy now, because I tell them that my phone is tapped, that the government's watching me. But, you know, sometimes paranoia is justified. I get paid for doing nothing—even though I've called many times and said I don't deserve disability pay. So I decided to use the money to do research, to study physics. . . ."

"*Physics?*" Katherine repeated. Clearly, that wasn't what she'd expected.

"Well, yeah . . ." Angela looked down at her hands. Jonah noticed she had her fingers knotted together, like she was suddenly very tense. "Look, you're not going to believe me anyhow, so maybe I shouldn't even tell you this part. I've been working on this for thirteen years, and it's gotten me nothing but scorn and mockery. And I've gotten no confirmation—no sign that what I believe is true. At least, not since that first day. So maybe I should just pat your heads, and tell you to run off and be good little children for your parents, and don't worry about where you came from. Don't be like me, obsessed and paranoid and—"

"We already are," Chip said firmly. "It's too late."

Speak for yourself! Jonah thought. But he was dying to hear Angela's theory too. He couldn't walk away now either.

Angela took a deep breath.

"Okay, then," she said. "One thing I saw that nobody else did—though I did report it when I was debriefed, before they began talking about confidentiality statements—was an insignia on the plane. By the time everyone else saw the plane, it looked like any other Sky Trails regional jet. But when I first saw it, the plane's door said, TACHYON TRAVEL. *Tachyon—T-A-C-H-Y-O-N.* You're all too young, probably, to have studied much physics—and anyway, this is very theoretical physics—"

"So what's a tachyon?" Katherine asked. She always hated being talked down to or told that she was too young for something.

"Tachyons are particles that travel faster than the speed of light," Angela said.

The speed of light? Jonah thought. *What's that got to do with anything?*

"I thought nothing could travel faster than light," Katherine said, acting proud that she knew that.

"Nobody knows really," Angela said. She was speaking very carefully now, watching for their reactions. "At least, nobody knows *yet*. The theories are that if anything could go faster than light, all sorts of weird things would happen. Time and space would have a different relationship. Aging would be different. And, if a plane could travel that fast, it'd become . . . a time machine."

Everyone stared at her.

Chip was already shaking his head.

"Who'd send a bunch of babies in a time machine?" he asked scornfully. "What would be the point?"

"I don't think anyone sent a bunch of babies in a time machine," Angela said, speaking very precisely. "I think a bunch of adults got into a time machine. I think it was an experiment, one of the first attempts at time travel. They didn't understand all the effects. So they didn't realize what would happen when they arrived in our time." She paused, letting that sink in.

"You mean—" Katherine asked.

Jonah couldn't tell if she really understood or if she was just prompting Angela.

"I mean that Chip and Jonah used to be much older than they are now," Angela said. "I think they were changed by traveling through time. I think they—and all the other babies—came from the future."

NINETEEN

Silence. Dead silence.

Jonah wasn't really even thinking about what Angela had said, because it was too bizarre and incredible to consider. It was like his brain shut down, rejecting her theory so completely. After a few moments, he thought to look at Chip and Katherine to see how they were reacting—mostly he was concerned that they'd be all rude and mocking and mean to Angela, when clearly she was just a nutcase. Oh, sure, she'd seemed fairly reasonable at first, except for being scared to talk on the telephone. But believing in time travel? And babies aging backward? Insanity.

Chip and Katherine both had their mouths open already, though Chip's might have just been hanging open in shock.

"Well, thanks for meeting with us," Jonah said quickly, hoping he could get everyone away from Angela before Katherine had a chance to speak. "Your ideas are, um, very interesting." He was struggling for words, trying to think of a polite excuse to leave. Could he carry off, *Oh, my, look at the time!*?

Suddenly something slammed into the glass door next to Jonah.

Instinctively, Jonah grabbed for the door handle, but it was too late. A man was wedging his heavily booted foot between the door and the glass wall. The rest of the man's body was sprawled out on the ground, because another man appeared to have tackled him.

"You can't do this!" the tackler was screaming. No, not exactly screaming. He was keeping his voice down, barely above a whisper, but his words still echoed with fury. "Not here. Not now. You'll make a scene. Do you want to ruin time completely?"

Jonah shoved against the man's boot; he drove his shoulder against the door, trying to shut it against the man's ankle. He couldn't see the man's face, because the tackler blocked his view. Then the tackler turned, and Jonah could at least see him clearly. A jolt of recognition flowed through his body; he was so stunned he almost let go of the door.

The tackler was the "janitor" from the FBI, the one who'd told Jonah to look at the file on Mr. Reardon's desk.

"Jonah! Chip! Run!" the tackler called urgently, struggling with the man in the boots.

What good was that? There was nowhere to run *to*, except out the door where the men were fighting. The booted man reared up, almost breaking the tackler's grip.

Katherine shrieked.

"The window!" Angela said.

She rushed over to the outer wall and began tugging on the window handle. Chip jumped up and helped her. The window opened inward, making a narrow V with the wall. Chip dived out through the small space, barely missing landing in a holly bush.

Katherine followed him quickly, executing a gymnastic-like move at the end, when she flipped over onto her feet.

"Jonah, come on!" she yelled in through the open window.

Jonah looked back at the men struggling on the ground. What would happen if he stopped holding the door?

"Go!" the tackler called over his shoulder.

Jonah ran for the window, skirting the table. He looked back once and saw that the men had rolled into the conference room. He still couldn't see the booted man's face, but he had a general impression of bulk, of muscles. He wasn't sure the tackler could hold him.

"You go first, Angela," Jonah said.

The name seemed to trigger a reaction in the tackler. He jerked his head back, looking over the top of the conference table.

"Angela DuPre," he called. "We have wronged you in time. We owe you—"

The tackler's head suddenly disappeared beneath the table. The booted man must have pulled him down. There was a sound like someone's head clunking against the floor, and the table lurched sideways.

"Angela?" Jonah urged.

He held out his hand to help her out of the window. She was wearing a skirt; she probably wouldn't want to go headfirst.

Angela drew back.

"You go on," she said. "I've been waiting thirteen years for something like this. I'm going to stick around and get some answers."

"But they're dangerous!" Jonah protested. He couldn't see the men at all now, but he could hear them, grunting and punching and slamming into the chairs and the table.

"Probably. That's why *you* need to get out of here," Angela said. She pushed him toward the window. He grabbed on to the frame, spreading his fingers against the glass to brace himself as he slid his feet out.

"Go, Jonah!" the tackler called from beneath the table. "Hurry! And Jonah—I saw your note! You have to be careful! Careful where you leave anything that could be seen later . . . anything that could be monitored—"

That was all Jonah heard, because he was out the window now, and the tackler was still using that low voice of hushed urgency. Jonah looked back, and he could see the tackler clearly now, under the table. He had one hand pressed into the other man's hair, holding his head down. With his other hand, the tackler was frantically waving Jonah away. His mouth formed the words, "Go! Go! Now!" But Jonah couldn't really hear him.

Jonah spun around and ran. He quickly caught up with Chip and Katherine. Without even speaking, all three of them ran for the bike rack, scooped up their bikes, and took off, pedaling furiously.

They were halfway down the bike path before Jonah's mind kicked into gear, letting him think again instead of just acting on reflex.

He immediately slammed on his brakes.

TWENTY

Katherine was the first to notice that Jonah wasn't keeping up, that he wasn't pedaling hysterically toward home alongside her and Chip.

"Jonah!" she called over her shoulder from several bike-lengths ahead. "What are you doing?"

"I have to go back!" he yelled. "We can't just leave Angela like that!"

"But—she's a grown-up! She told us to go!" This was Chip arguing now.

"She—"

Jonah decided he didn't have time to stand there and argue. He whirled around and began pedaling back toward the library just as desperately as he'd been pedaling away from it.

Grown-ups can get kidnapped too, he thought. *And she's a little nutty, she'd probably trust anyone who pretended to believe her crazy theories. . . . Her theories are just craziness, aren't they?*

Jonah couldn't think about that right now. He focused on trying to pedal faster. By the time he reached the library, his legs were aching and he was gasping for air. He dropped his bike on the sidewalk and slipped in the door just ahead of a mother pushing a baby stroller and holding a toddler's hand and taking infuriatingly slow steps, with a play-by-play commentary: "That's right, you push the button for the automatic door opener and then the door will open, and . . ."

Jonah dashed through the lobby, past the check-out desk.

"Young man! No running in the library!"

It was a librarian, one of the women his mom always said hello to when she stopped in. Jonah thought maybe this librarian had been in charge of story hour when he and Katherine were preschoolers.

"I just—the conference room—men fighting—danger—"

That was all Jonah could manage, with his lungs threatening to burst.

To her credit, the librarian stopped yelling and sprang into action.

"Show me," she said.

She rushed along behind Jonah, practically running herself.

They dashed through the stacks, past the magazine section where Katherine had hidden before, past the nonfiction shelves with all the thick books about taxes. Then, finally, Jonah could see into the conference room and—

It was empty.

"Angela?" Jonah called.

He pushed his way into the conference room. Not only was the room empty, but all the chairs were lined up perfectly around the table. And the table was exactly centered in the room, as if it had never been knocked off-kilter by struggling men. The window was closed. The only sign that anything had happened here was a smudge on the glass wall—probably Jonah's own fingerprints, smeared against the glass when he'd scrambled out a window.

"Just what did you think was going on in here?" the librarian asked. She had her eyebrows raised doubtfully.

Just then Jonah saw a movement out of the corner of his eye. He turned his head to peer out the window, and there was Angela. She was walking briskly through the far end of the parking lot.

"That's the woman!" Jonah exclaimed. "The one who was in danger—"

While Jonah was watching, Angela stepped into the cluster of pine trees on the other side of the parking lot. She turned and lifted her hand in a way that might have been a wave at Jonah. And then she just . . . vanished.

Jonah hadn't known that it would look like that. He'd heard Katherine's description of the janitor appearing and disappearing; he'd heard Angela's description of the plane doing the same thing. But he hadn't understood how strange it would be, how it would set every nerve in his body on edge and make him question all sorts of basic tenets about how the world worked. Could gravity be tampered with too? Could . . . time?

Jonah blinked and stared and stammered, "But—but—" and then he at least had the sense to shut his mouth, because the librarian was looking at him oddly. Already his brain was trying to supply explanations for him—*She just stepped behind a tree. . . . You just blinked and thought you saw something odd*—the same kind of explanations he'd tried to use to account for Katherine's story, for Angela's. The kind of explanation anyone else, casually glancing out a window, would have accepted without a second thought. But his glance hadn't been casual: he knew he hadn't blinked, not while Angela was disappearing. He understood now what Angela had meant when she had said, "I know what I saw. I trust my own eyes." The scene had been clear and distinct, and he really had seen Angela vanish into thin air.

"Where is this woman?" the librarian asked. "I don't quite see—"

"She's gone."

The librarian narrowed her eyes at him and tilted her head suspiciously.

"So, what was this?" she asked. "A dare? Your audition for drama club? If so, I heartily recommend you for whatever part you're trying out for, because you really had me convinced—you had *me* running through the library."

"I wasn't lying!" Jonah protested. "There really were two men in here fighting, and they seemed dangerous, and—"

The librarian tapped her chin, her eyes narrowing further.

"How did you see what was going on in this conference room *before* you ran in the front door?" she asked.

"Um, through the glass? From outside?" Jonah said, which did have a grain of truth to it. Still, his words came out sounding like a question.

"Someone did mention that they thought they heard a girl scream back here, but we thought it was just one of those computer games. . . ." The librarian seemed to be talking mostly to herself. She reached out and grabbed Jonah's arm. "Come with me. We'll do a search through the library and you tell me if you see either of those men."

Meekly, Jonah let himself be led back through the magazine section, past the row of computers, past the reference desk, through the little-kid section where the mother with the toddler was asking with exaggerated patience, "What will it be? *Curious George* or *The Cat in the Hat?*"

In the YA section, some kids from school were playing on the computers, and they pointed and giggled when they saw Jonah being paraded around, his arm trapped in the librarian's grip.

"I don't see either of the men now," Jonah said, his face burning with shame. He just wanted to get out of the library, away from the librarian. He could see Chip and Katherine standing hesitantly by the front door, as if they weren't sure if they needed to come and rescue him or not.

The librarian let go of his arm.

"I think you did see *something*," she muttered. "You really were looking carefully for those men."

And Jonah had been. Even when the kids from school had been laughing at him, he'd made sure that he peered down every aisle between the bookshelves, every nook of the little-kid reading area.

The men were nowhere in sight.

"Oh, well," Jonah said, trying very hard to keep his

voice from shaking. "Nothing's wrong now. Can I just go?"

The librarian regarded him thoughtfully.

"Go on, then," she said.

Jonah could feel her eyes on him as he went to join Chip and Katherine. Walking out the door, he felt robotic, because his body was doing something so normal—one foot stepping in front of the other, hands held out to shove against the door—while his mind was zipping and zooming and alighting on one strange thought after the other.

"What happened?" Katherine asked. "Is Angela okay?"

"Angela . . ." Jonah had to struggle so hard to focus his mind, to concentrate on the one precise moment of memory that his brain kept trying to transform into something normal and acceptable, something that would fit with everything else he already knew about the world. He wouldn't let his brain do that; he wouldn't stop trusting his own eyes.

"I saw Angela," Jonah said. "I don't know if she's okay or not. I think she went into a time warp."

TWENTY-ONE

"Not you, too!" Chip complained.

"I'm sorry!" Jonah said. He bent over, bracing his hands against his knees, trying to pull more air into his lungs, a delayed reaction to all his frantic pedaling and running. As soon as he could, he looked back up at Chip. "I'm not *sure* that's what happened. I'm not sure of anything anymore. But I *think* that's what happened, because it makes the most sense."

"The most sense?" Chip repeated in amazement. "That's the *best* explanation you can come up with? A time warp?"

"You didn't see what I saw," Jonah said. The edges of his vision were a little blurry even now, but this was a normal feeling. *Oxygen deprivation*, his mind automatically labeled it. He felt the way he did after he'd played an entire soccer game as midfielder, running up and down the field for a solid hour. He'd felt this way after the soccer game this morning.

Oh, jeez, he thought. *I played that soccer game and then I rode my bike like a maniac—no wonder I feel so dead. No wonder I'm seeing things. I mean, not seeing things. Seeing someone vanish. Or, wait . . . maybe she wasn't really there in the first place?*

His thoughts got so tangled that his mind gave up trying to revise his memory of seeing Angela vanish. It had happened. Period.

"Katherine," he gasped. "When you said you saw the janitor disappear—I shouldn't have made fun of you. I didn't know. . . ."

"You believe me now?" Katherine asked. "Why?" Comprehension dawned on her face. "Angela disappeared, didn't she? And you saw it. . . ."

Jonah nodded.

"I'll show you."

He started to stumble over something—it was his own bike, where he'd dropped it in the middle of the sidewalk. He picked it up, and then it was nice to have the handlebars to lean on as he led Chip and Katherine through the parking lot, over to the cluster of pine trees. He dropped his bike again by the curb.

"She was right here," he said, stepping into the pine

needles. "I saw her. And then she took one step forward"—
he took a step—"and she was gone."

Jonah rocked back on his heels, stepped forward again.
He felt nothing different in either place. There was no tem-
perature change, no wind howling furiously around some
time portal. In both spots—before his step and after—he
felt just a gentle breeze, the sunshine warm on the back of
his neck, the pine needles soft beneath his feet.

"Guess the time warp only wanted Angela, not you,"
Chip said mockingly, but there was an edge of fear in his
voice.

"Or—someone's protecting you," Katherine said.

Jonah looked at his sister. She was in the middle of
pulling her hair back, capturing it in a ponytail. Jonah
was surprised to see how red her face was. She had a ring
of sweat where her bike helmet had pressed against her
head, and the sweat was trickling down her cheeks. He
was amazed that she was willing to be seen in public like
this.

"Didn't you notice," she began in an oddly strangled
voice, "how, when those men were fighting, the cute janitor guy yelled out, 'Jonah! Chip! Run!'? He didn't say *my*
name. He didn't say Angela's."

"You think those guys were fighting over *us*?" Chip
asked. "Why not you, too?"

"You're the babies from the plane," Katherine said. "I'm not."

Jonah thought about this. The fight and the fleeing had happened so fast, all he had were jumbled images in his head. But the janitor/tackler had seemed to be trying to protect them.

"How did he know our names?" he asked. "Mine, I guess from Mr. Reardon's office, but—Chip's?" He remembered something else. "And he did recognize Angela. I don't know if you two heard, because you were out the window already, but he called her Angela DuPre. And he said—he said—" It was such a struggle to remember, "—something like, 'We have wronged you.' No, 'We have wronged you in time. We owe you.'"

"'In time'?" Chip whispered.

Katherine sat down on the curb, her elbows propped on her knees, her face caught in her hands.

"That whole plane thing did kind of ruin Angela's life," she said. "I mean, refusing to talk on the telephone? Having everyone think she's crazy?"

Chip sat down beside Katherine.

"What does the janitor guy have to do with the plane?" he asked. "And who was the guy he was fighting with? What did he want to do to us?"

Jonah stiffened.

"Beware," he quoted. "They're coming back to get you. That's what the letter said. That's who they were warning us about!"

He looked around frantically. What if the man tried again, sometime when no one was around to protect them?

Katherine shook her head, her ponytail flipping back and forth.

"Really," she said disgustedly, "if the cute janitor wanted to warn you, he should have provided a few more details. Names, dates—something you could go to the police with."

"The police would never believe this," Chip groaned. "*I* don't even believe it!"

Jonah could feel the sweat rolling down his back. But it wasn't leftover sweat from all his biking and running. It was new sweat, panicky sweat, proof that his body thought he should be completely terrified.

"Well, here's what we need to do," Katherine said, tossing her head emphatically, her ponytail whipping out behind her. "We need to call all the other kids on the survivors list again and see if they've had any experiences with some guy trying to catch them or some other guy trying to protect them. We need to gather some data—see if any of them have ever seen someone just vanish into thin air. *And* we need to warn them, to let them know what we know."

"But we don't know anything," Chip said.

"We know about the plane," Katherine said. "We know where Angela thinks the plane came from. We know what janitor boy looks like. We know what one of your letters means."

Tallied up that way, Katherine's plan almost sounded reasonable. She sounded as calm as Mom always did, dealing with a crisis. One time, when Jonah was little, he'd dropped a glass and it had shattered on the kitchen floor. And Mom had been there immediately, telling him in her most soothing voice, "Yes, Jonah, I see that there's glass all over the floor and I see that you're barefoot, and that is a little bit scary. But if you just stand there like a statue, I'll pick you up and you'll be fine and then I'll sweep up all the glass. . . ."

Jonah had escaped without a single cut. If Katherine could master that same voice now, he was willing to let her take control.

"All right," he said.

Chip shrugged. "Whatever."

All three of them retrieved their bikes and began walking them back toward the bike path. Chip and Katherine hadn't played a soccer game or pedaled quite as frantically as Jonah had earlier, but neither of them seemed any more eager than he was to speed home. They rode slowly, each of them stopping at various points to say, "If there really is such a thing as time travel . . ." or "if we really are from the future . . ." or "if that plane was a time machine . . ."

None of them seemed capable of making a complete sentence, of following any of the "ifs" to a logical conclusion.

That's because there aren't any logical conclusions, Jonah told himself. He'd read time-travel books, he'd seen time-travel movies, and they'd always seemed wrong to him. Couldn't the people just keep going back again and again and again, keep changing time until it turned out the way they wanted it to? And there was some paradox he remembered hearing about, something about a grandmother—oh, yeah, time travel had to be impossible because, otherwise, you could go back in time and kill your own grandmother. But if you killed your own grandmother, then you wouldn't exist, so you couldn't go back in time, so your grandmother would be alive again, but then you would also exist again, so you could go back and kill your grandmother, but then you would never be born. . . .

Jonah's head hurt just thinking about it.

They reached Chip's house and actually parked their bikes neatly in the driveway. Even though they'd ridden slowly, Jonah was still drenched with sweat.

"Hey, I'm really rank," he said. "Unless you want me stinking up your whole basement, I'd better take a shower before we start calling people."

Katherine sniffed.

"Uh, me too," she said. She didn't have Mom's authoritative voice anymore; she just sounded embarrassed.

"Okay," Chip said. "But hurry back."

He sounded like he didn't want to be left alone, but he was too ashamed to say so.

Jonah and Katherine took their bikes back to their own garage.

"You can have the shower in Mom and Dad's bathroom," Katherine said, not quite looking at him. This was a gift on her part—probably a sign that she felt sorry for him—because Mom and Dad's bathroom was bigger and nicer than the one between his and Katherine's rooms. Usually she'd dash into the better bathroom ahead of him, slamming the door shut, jabbing the lock, and shrieking, "Ha, ha, ha! Beat you! You snooze, you lose!"

"Thanks," Jonah mumbled.

He didn't care about where he took his shower right now.

In the shower he stood under the pounding spray for a long time after he'd soaped and rinsed off. The hot water felt good, even though Mom and Dad were always nagging about not wasting water and energy.

"You kids should be concerned about the future," Mom always said, "because you're going to have to live there. . . ."

"Oh, no," Jonah moaned. Was that what this was about? In so many of the time-travel books and movies he'd seen, people came back from the future to warn about global warming or stuff like that. What if he and Jonah and the other kids were supposed to deliver some message about how people needed to make big changes now to save the world in the future?

"Lots of people are already talking about global warming," he said aloud, even though he wasn't sure whom he was talking to. "Nobody's going to listen to me."

Also, if this was an environmental thing, what were the two sides fighting over? Did the janitor just want him to stay here to deliver his message? Did the other guy want the world to end?

Jonah wasn't enjoying his shower anymore. He shut off the water, stepped out, and pulled a towel from the rack. Distantly, he heard the phone ringing. Then it stopped ringing—Dad must have gotten up from watching the Ohio State game to answer it. Jonah knew Katherine would still be in the shower because she always took forever. Then she always had to spend another eternity drying her hair—she'd be doing well to make it back to Chip's house before midnight.

"Jonah?" It was Dad, shouting up the stairs. "Chip's on the phone. He says it's urgent. Can you get the phone up there?"

"Sure," Jonah said.

He wrapped the towel around his waist and went for the phone in his parents' bedroom.

"Got it, Dad," Jonah yelled. He heard the click that meant Dad had hung up downstairs. "Hello?"

"They're gone," Chip said, his voice cracking.

"What's gone?"

"The lists on my computer—the survivors list, the witnesses list, the files where Katherine and I were keeping checklists about who said what—it all disappeared. But the rest of the computer is fine. How could that be?" Chip's voice arced toward hysteria.

"Calm down," Jonah said. "Maybe you just deleted something by mistake. Did you check in the *Delete* file?"

"Not there."

"Didn't you have everything backed up?"

Silence. Evidently Chip didn't.

"But you made printouts," Jonah reminded him.

"I left them at the library," Chip groaned. "I didn't get them back from Angela before we climbed out the window—did you pick them up? Did Katherine?"

Jonah thought about this. He could remember the papers

lying on the table in front of Angela, right before the first man slammed against the door. What had happened to the lists after that? When he'd run around the table to get to the window, had the breeze lifted the pages slightly into the air? After he'd climbed out the window and glanced back, had the papers been sliding across the table, as the fighting men jolted it from below? Why hadn't he paid more attention? And why hadn't he simply grabbed the papers as he ran?

"There wasn't time!" Jonah said, his voice unnecessarily surly.

"Maybe if I call the library," Chip said desperately, "maybe somebody found them—"

"Don't bother," Jonah said. "They weren't there when I went back." He was sure of that detail.

"Do you think Angela took them?" Chip asked.

Jonah shrugged, forgetting that Chip couldn't see him.

"What good does that do us?" Jonah said. He didn't want to speculate about where Angela might have gone with the papers. A new thought occurred to him. "Doesn't Katherine still have all the pictures stored on her cell phone?"

"She deleted them after we downloaded everything," Chip moaned. "She said they took up too much space, and she was worried that your parents might see them, because sometimes your mom borrows that phone. . . ."

This was true. Mom had been having trouble with her own phone battery.

Some of Chip's despair was beginning to infect Jonah.

"Then we don't have anything left from those lists at all?" Jonah asked, his own voice edging toward panic. "Nothing?"

"I still have Daniella McCarthy's phone number on my cell," Chip offered.

"But no one else's?"

"I used our home phone for everyone else," Chip said. "Katherine told me I was being mean, trying to rack up all those minutes on my cell."

And you actually listened to her? Jonah wanted to scream. Instead he squeezed his eyes shut. *Stay calm*, he ordered himself.

"Your parents," he began slowly. "If they don't want to talk about you being adopted—do you think they might have deleted those files? Do you think if maybe you go ask them—?"

"My parents never look at my computer," Chip said bitterly. "They don't care. The only people who knew about those files were you and Katherine and me. And I didn't tell anyone. Did you? Did Katherine?"

"No," Jonah said automatically. But he still had his eyes squeezed shut, and it was as if he had his memory displayed on the backs of his eyelids: he could see his own hand sweeping across a page, writing out, "All the information is on Chip's computer, in the basement at his house."

"Oh, no," Jonah said. His eyes sprang open again, and he caught a glimpse of his own stricken expression in his parents' dresser mirror. "The note. The note I left for my parents when we went to the library, just in case something happened . . ."

"Did they read it?" Chip asked, horrified. "You think they came over and erased my computer files? Would they do that?"

"No. . . ." But Jonah took the phone and rushed down the hall to his own room. The note was still hidden in the top drawer of his desk, right beside the mysterious letter, *Beware! They're coming back to get you.* He thought about the casual way Dad had shouted up the stairs about the phone call—Dad hadn't seen this note. And Mom was still out running errands. She hadn't seen it either.

Then he remembered the man at the library, struggling under the table as Jonah scrambled out the window.

Go, Jonah! Hurry! And Jonah—I saw your note! You have to be careful! Careful where you leave anything that could be seen later . . . anything that could be monitored—

"Oh, no," Jonah moaned. "It was one of them."

"Them who?"

But Jonah was peering suspiciously around his room. It looked like usual, the NBA poster a little crooked on the wall, the blue bedspread slightly rumpled, the closet door open a crack with his shoes half-in and half-out. It was all so familiar. But it had been invaded at least twice now, that he knew of. The very air seemed to crackle with danger.

Except—was it really dangerous right this minute? If people could just appear anywhere they wanted (and he was still trying to get his mind around that idea), why didn't someone just grab him now? Why hadn't they taken him back with the plane, or during any one of the thousands of seconds of his life since then?

Maybe time travel wasn't so easy.

Be careful! Careful where you leave anything that could be seen later . . . anything that could be monitored—

Seen later. Monitored . . . Maybe the next word after that would have been *later* too. Maybe, if time travel even existed, there were limits to it. Maybe it was something about the rotation of the earth, or sunspots, or something bizarre like that. So anything written down was dangerous, because it could be seen at any time. And other things, things that could be monitored were cell phone pictures, and computer hard drives, and . . .

Jonah gasped.

"Chip, I can't tell you anything right now. Not over the phone."

"Why not?" Chip demanded. "This is crazy—you're starting to sound like Angela."

"What if Angela's right?"

TWENTY-TWO

Jonah, Chip, and Katherine slumped in various chairs in Chip's basement.

"Is this safe?" Katherine asked. "Talking together here now?"

"I don't know," Jonah said miserably. "How long do sound waves stay in the air?"

"I can check online," Chip said. He turned around to the computer and began to type in, *How long do . . .*

"Chip, someone could check your search record, find out that you asked that question," Jonah objected.

"So what? I could just be doing science homework," Chip said. But he stopped typing. The words *How long do* stayed on the computer screen.

How long do we have to figure everything out? Jonah wondered. *How long do we have before someone appears out of nowhere and carries us away?*

He'd finally told Chip and Katherine about seeing an intruder in his room, the night they'd first gotten the lists of witnesses and survivors. Then he'd explained his theory about how someone—the janitor? The janitor's enemy?—had found out about Chip's computer files from the note in Jonah's desk. And how, if he—whoever "he" was—could find Jonah's note and Chip's computer files, then that person could just as easily tap their phones. For all Jonah knew, someone could have gone back in time to tap their phones ten years ago, but was listening to their conversations fifty years in the future.

Jonah was beginning to feel hopeless. How could you resist someone with that kind of power?

"All right," Katherine said briskly. "Let's assume that talking is safe because, if it isn't, we can't do anything. Chip, do you have any paper?"

"Katherine, I told you—they can read anything we write down!"

Katherine rolled her eyes and reached down to pull a sheet of paper out of Chip's printer. She snagged a pen out of the middle of a stack of computer games and dodged Jonah's hands when he tried to pull the pen away from her.

"I know, I know," she said impatiently. "I'll destroy the evidence as soon as I'm done. I'll eat the paper if I have to. But we have to get organized!"

She bent over the computer desk and wrote two headings on the top of her paper: *What we know* and *What we think.* She drew a line down the middle of the page, dividing the two topics. Under *What we know,* she wrote, *JB gave us witnesses/survivors lists.* And then under *What we think,* she added, *So JB's probably not the one who took them away.*

"JB?" Chip asked.

"Janitor boy," Katherine said. "I would have called him CJB for 'cute janitor boy,' but that's just my opinion, and probably not how you and Jonah think about him, so—"

"Katherine!" Jonah growled through gritted teeth. He pointed to the list. "Focus!"

Katherine grinned triumphantly, not looking chastised at all. Dimly, Jonah realized that she may have been *trying* to aggravate him, to jolt him out of his gloom. She shook her wet hair gleefully, sending out drops of water all over the paper.

Wait a minute—had Katherine really agreed to come down here to Chip's without blow-drying her hair first? Jonah hadn't noticed before, because he'd been so freaked out. But this undoubtedly meant that Katherine *didn't* have a crush on Chip. Or, if she did, she thought this mystery was more important . . .

Jonah decided to apply his brainpower to Katherine's list instead of her love interests.

"JB was trying to protect us from E," he said, pointing to the *What we know* column. "And E stands for *enemy*."

Nobody argued with him.

"Okay," Katherine said after a pause, and wrote it down.

"We need another category," Chip said. "*What we don't know*—why was JB protecting us? What did E want to do with us?"

He pulled out another sheet and handed it to Katherine. None of them commented on the fact that *What we don't know* got a whole sheet of paper, while *What we know* and *What we think* got only a half sheet apiece.

JB tried to warn Jonah went into the *know* category, but they all agreed that *the phones are tapped* only qualified for *What we think*.

"Angela vanished into thin air," Jonah said. "Know."

He was glad that Chip didn't challenge that one.

Without asking, Katherine added *into a time warp?* and *with our lists* under *What we think*.

"And then under *What we don't know*, you can add about a billion questions," Chip said. "How? Why? How did she know the time warp was there? How did she go through it today when she'd been studying time travel for thirteen years and hadn't gotten anywhere?"

Katherine chewed on the pen thoughtfully.

"I bet JB helped her," she said.

"But Jonah would have seen JB if he'd been there with her," Chip objected.

"Maybe he told her how the time warp worked," Katherine said. "Or . . . maybe he was invisible."

Invisible? Jonah thought. *We've got to worry about invisible people too?*

"Angela didn't look upset or anything," Jonah said. On the contrary, when he pictured her stepping into nothingness, re-living that moment he'd already re-lived so many times already, he thought she'd had an excited expression on her face. Or . . . determined. "But—maybe we should call her. Just to make sure. And to see if she has our lists."

"Call her?" Chip asked. "Fifteen minutes ago, you wouldn't even talk to me on the phone!"

"I know, but if we're careful about what we say, just kind of hint that we want to meet with her again, to find out what happened, to see if she has our lists. . . . Hand me the cell phone, Katherine," Jonah said.

Katherine dug the phone out of her pocket and handed it over.

"We don't have her phone number anymore, remember?" Chip said.

"I'll call information," Jonah said. He was already starting to punch in numbers.

Katherine scrunched up her face, like she was thinking hard.

"She lives on Stonehenge," she said. "Stonehenge Court or Street or something like that—I remember thinking that someone involved in a mystery should have a mysterious address like that."

"Thanks," Jonah said. To the operator, he said, "I need the number for an Angela or A. DuPre on Stonehenge—DuPre—D-U-P-R-E."

"Thank you," the operator said. And then, a second later, "I don't have a listing for any A. or Angela DuPre anywhere in the city."

"But I know she's there!" Jonah protested.

"Maybe her number's unlisted," the operator said. "Or she just uses a cell phone. Lots of people are doing that now, and they're not in the directory."

It would be like Angela to have an unlisted number, Jonah thought.

"Thanks anyway," he said, and cut off the call.

Chip and Katherine were staring, like they were worried about him now.

"It doesn't matter," Chip joked. "She's probably not back from the time warp anyhow."

"Maybe, maybe not," Katherine said. "You could go through a time warp, and stay in the other time for thirty years, and then return just a split second after you left."

"I was still watching a split second after she left," Jonah said grumpily. "She didn't come back."

Not being able to find Angela's number bothered him more than it should have. It was like he didn't have control over anything.

"Okay, then," Katherine said, with forced cheer. "How about all the stuff Angela told us about the plane and the babies? And—her theory about you two being from the future?"

"That's all impossible," Chip said. "Isn't it?"

And yet, they'd sort of begun treating it like it was real, like they believed it.

"Why would anyone come back from the future to now?" Jonah asked. "What's happening now that matters? And here—in Ohio?"

"Yeah," Katherine said. "If you're going to go back in time, you save Abraham Lincoln from being assassinated. Or John F. Kennedy. Or, you keep the *Titanic* from sinking. Or you stop 9/11. Or—I know—you assassinate Hitler before he has a chance to start World War II."

"Or you bet on who's going to win the World Series, which you already know because—duh!—you're from the future," Chip said. "Or you invest in Microsoft stock before anybody's ever heard of Microsoft."

Jonah shrugged.

"Maybe there's something big that's about to happen here that we don't know about," he said. He saw Katherine trying to suppress a shiver. "What I don't get is why there are two sides fighting over us." He looked down at Katherine's list, which was full of *JB*'s and *E*'s. "What do they want from us?"

"And how can we find out before it's too late?" Katherine asked.

TWENTY-THREE

They were stymied.

For the next week, practically every day, one of them had a brainstorm.

On Monday, Katherine thought of actually walking or riding their bikes to visit every single kid in Liston they remembered being on their list. But they couldn't remember very many street names, and the ones they remembered turned out to be way over on the other side of the highway, too far away.

On Tuesday, Jonah thought of calling other DuPres to ask them if they knew Angela, and, if so, if she was all right.

"JB and E already know that we know Angela," he argued with Chip and Katherine. "They saw us talking to her. What could it hurt if they find out that we're looking for her again?"

His arguments didn't matter—the only DuPre he could find from directory assistance had just moved from Louisiana and had never heard of Angela.

On Wednesday, Chip said, "That's it. I'm calling Daniella McCarthy back. I don't care who hears me."

But her phone rang and rang and rang, and then a computerized message clicked on: "This phone has been disconnected." There was no other number given.

"Ergh!" Chip kicked his desk chair, and sent it spiraling across the basement floor. "They probably canceled their landline and went down to just cell phones during the move. That's what we did—oh, why didn't I call her back last week?" He pounded his fists on the desk.

On Thursday, Katherine thought of riding their bikes slowly down Robin's Egg Lane, looking for FOR SALE or SOLD signs or—if they got really lucky—moving vans. They did find a McCoy Realty sign stuck in the yard at 1873, which *sounded* right to Jonah and Chip. But when they knocked at the door, the sound echoed vacantly. All the windows were covered with blinds, so they couldn't see in.

A woman stepped out on the porch across the street.

"Nobody's going to buy your band's candy or raffle tickets or whatever it is you're trying to sell there," she said. "That house has been empty for months. And while we're at it, I don't want to buy anything either."

"Oh, we're not selling anything," Katherine said quickly.

Jonah jabbed his elbow into her ribs, because what if the woman jumped to a worse conclusion? What if she thought they were planning to break in?

Katherine ignored him.

"We're just from the, uh, middle school Welcome Wagon," she said. "We had information that a thirteen-year-old girl was moving in here, and we came to make sure that she feels comfortable in Liston. Do we have our dates wrong? Do you know when the McCarthys are moving in?"

"Well, I wouldn't know anything about that," the woman said. "I do seem to remember hearing something about the paperwork on that house being messed up, delaying everything—but, of course, it's none of my business." She gave them a sharp look. "Or yours."

Friday afternoon, Jonah shoved aside his math homework and wrote on a clean sheet of paper:

JB,
We could use a little help here. Hints? Clues? Can't you tell us anything?

Then he tore the paper into pieces and threw it in the

trash can beside his desk, because how would JB know that they called him JB? And what if E found the note instead?

It was a good thing that he'd destroyed the evidence so quickly, because a few moments later his mom poked her head in his door.

"Jonah, I didn't want to bring this up in front of Katherine, but we got this flyer in the mail today." She held out a glossy sheet of paper. Halfway across the room, Jonah could read the title: *Adoptees on the Cusp of Their Teen Years . . . a Conference for Adolescents and Their Parents.*

"It's part of a series put on by the county department of social services," she said. "This conference is just for families in Liston and Clarksville and Upper Tyson, so it probably wouldn't be a huge crowd. You've just been acting so . . . disturbed lately, ever since we met with Mr. Reardon. Not that I blame you—I was disturbed by that man too! But even before that, you were asking questions about your adoption. . . . All the books say the teen years are when a lot of adoptees begin struggling with their identities. I think we should go to this. You and Dad and me."

Liston and Clarksville and Upper Tyson, Jonah thought. *Perfect.*

"Okay," Jonah said, trying very hard to hide his eagerness.

He needed to sound reluctant, put-upon—maybe even still disturbed. He tried to sound as if something new had just occurred to him, as if he didn't much care: "Oh—could we make a copy of that? I think Chip and his parents will want to go too."

TWENTY-FOUR

"What if it's a trap?" Katherine asked.

"How could it be a trap?" Jonah asked. "It's sponsored by the county."

The two of them were rather listlessly playing basketball in the driveway. Mom had shooed them outside—"Go! Get some fresh air! You've both been so mopey lately. I don't think you're getting enough exercise!" So they were standing under the hoop, but they kept forgetting to bounce the ball, to shoot it.

Chip was at a dentist's appointment, so they hadn't been able to share the news about the conference with him yet.

"The county," Katherine snorted, giving the ball a hard shove toward Chip. "Yeah, and we got the list of survivors and witnesses from the FBI, which is also the *government*.

How do you know that E didn't set this whole thing up?"

How do we know that the government's not involved in every-thing? Jonah thought. *How do we know that they didn't help E tap our phones? How do we know that the time travelers—JB or E or both of them—can't manipulate the government however they want to? How do we know that anything's safe?*

He didn't care anymore. He was going to the conference, no matter what. He was sick of feeling stymied.

What he said to Katherine was, "I went back and looked at the county Web site—the conference has been on their schedule for more than a year. It'd be hard to set that up as a trap."

"The county Web site?" Katherine's eyes bugged out a little. "So you left a trail on our computer. . . ."

"Don't worry, I went back in and cleared the browsing history," Jonah said. "A kid at school showed me how to do that."

He shot the ball with exaggerated swagger, false confidence. The ball sailed through the hoop, but Jonah had the feeling that it could just as easily have bounced off.

Just as the conference could be a trap.

"I don't like it," Katherine said, grabbing the rebound. "It just seems too convenient that it's for Liston and Clarksville and Upper Tyson, and those are the same places where all the kids on the survivors list moved."

"But it will be a perfect opportunity to talk to some of the kids from the list—I'm sure at least some of them will be there. You do remember the names, don't you?" Jonah said.

"Sure," Katherine said. "Andrea Crowell. Haley Rivers. Michael Kostoff." She began bouncing the ball in time with the names. "Sarah Puchini. Josh Hart. Rusty Devorall. Anthony Solbers. Uh—" The ball landed on her foot and began rolling down the driveway. She waited while Jonah chased the ball out into the street. "Chip probably remembers the other names, or we'd remember them if we heard them."

"Wait a minute," Jonah said, running back. He bounced the ball back to Katherine, a little harder than necessary. "What do you mean, 'we'?"

Katherine took a shot. The ball swished cleanly through the net. She didn't even look surprised.

"I mean, I'm going too, of course," she said, grabbing her own rebound and holding on to it. "You and Chip will have to pretend to be paying attention to—what are some of the sessions called?—'Identity Issues for Teen Adoptees'? Or whatever. So you'll need me there too to get a chance to talk to all the other kids."

Jonah didn't want to admit it, but what she said made sense.

"How are we going to explain this to Mom and Dad?"

"Easy," Katherine said. She bounced the ball without looking at it. "You tell them you want me to come."

Jonah tried to steal the ball from her, but she saw him coming and jerked it out of reach.

"Now, how am I going to get them to believe that?" Jonah asked.

"You'll figure something out," Katherine said. She smiled sweetly. "That librarian thought you were a good actor."

When Jonah went back into the house, he saw that Mom had already written 9–3, *adoption conference* in the October 28 square on the kitchen calendar. Quickly he grabbed a pen and began inking over the words. He hadn't thought he'd have to worry about Mom and Dad's writing something that JB or E might see.

Mom came around the corner just as he'd managed to obliterate the last *e* of *conference*.

"Jonah—what are you doing?" she said, startled.

"I just, uh, started doodling," Jonah said. "Guess it got a little out of hand."

Mom looked completely bewildered.

"Even when you were a toddler, you didn't do things like that," she said.

"Mom, duh," Katherine said from across the kitchen, where she was pulling a Gatorade bottle from the refrigerator. Both Jonah and Mom turned to look at her. Somehow Katherine managed to roll her eyes and gulp down Gatorade at the same time. She lowered the bottle. "Think about it. If Jonah's suddenly all confused and worried about his identity, the last thing he needs is to have you write *adoption conference* in a public place like that."

"This isn't a public place," Mom said. "It's our kitchen."

"Yeah, but Rachel and Molly are in here all the time, and Chip, and all Jonah's other friends, and my other friends, and your friends, and Dad's friends. . . ." Katherine made it sound like thousands of people trooped through their kitchen every day.

"There's nothing wrong with the word *adoption*," Mom said defensively. "Or with being adopted."

"Yeah, but Jonah doesn't want it *advertised*," Katherine said. "Show some sensitivity. Jeez."

Mom turned her gaze from Katherine to Jonah and back again.

"I really thought Jonah was capable of speaking for himself," Mom said, suspicion creeping into her voice.

"Oh, he is," Katherine said sweetly. "Jonah, didn't you have something you wanted to ask Mom about the conference?"

Jonah shot Katherine a look that very clearly said, *I'm going to kill you when all this is over.* To Mom, he said, "Uh, yeah. I was just thinking, since Katherine seems to be having so many issues with *not* being adopted, that maybe she should go to the conference too. So she can find out what horrors she avoided by getting birth parents who were crazy enough to want to keep her."

"Oh, Jonah, that's not the way to look at this," Mom protested, at the same time that Katherine said, "Oh, could I go to the conference with you? That'd be great!"

Mom squinted at Jonah.

"Are you serious?" she asked.

It was really hard for Jonah to keep a straight face as he assured her, "Yep. Katherine wants to go to the conference, and I want her to go too."

"Could I? Please?" Katherine begged.

Mom frowned.

"Some days I can't figure out the two of you at all," she said.

Behind Mom's back, Katherine jerked her head at Jonah, as if to say, *Your turn. Close the deal!*

"So, can she come to the conference with us?" Jonah asked, trying to keep his eyes wide, his expression innocent.

"I suppose," Mom said. "Though I really don't understand why either of you wants this."

Katherine threw her arms around Mom's shoulders.

"Thanks, Mom," she said. "Just think—next year I'll be a teenager too, and then we'll really confuse you!"

TWENTY-FIVE

The next few weeks seemed to crawl by. Neither Chip nor Jonah got any more mysterious letters. Neither they nor Katherine saw anyone else appear out of nowhere or disappear into thin air. In fact, if it weren't for the butterflies that seemed to multiply in Jonah's stomach as October 28 approached, Jonah almost could have believed that his life had gone back to normal. He took another social studies test, about Mesopotamia and Babylon this time. He attended an informational meeting to find out about seventh-grade basketball tryouts. He went on a Boy Scout camp-out where it rained all weekend and two kids came down with bronchitis and coughed all night long, until the Scout leader gave in and called their parents at 5:00 a.m.

Katherine and Chip stayed obsessed.

"I figured out why you and Chip were adopted in

different states," Katherine announced one night as Jonah was brushing his teeth.

"Why?" Jonah said, through a mouthful of Crest.

"Think about it," Katherine said, loitering outside the bathroom. She spoke in a low voice, as if she were afraid that Mom and Dad might hear her from downstairs. "There were thirty-six babies. If Mr. Reardon had dumped you all on one adoption agency—or even several adoption agencies, all in the same city—there would have been a lot of talk. But you send one baby to Michigan, one or two to Chicago, one or two to Indianapolis . . . that's not so noticeable. There could be that many abandoned babies in each city at once."

Jonah spit into the sink, bending low so she didn't see how the word *abandoned* stabbed at him.

I wasn't abandoned, he reminded himself. *I was sent. On a plane.*

But was that better or worse than being abandoned?

"So do you think Mr. Reardon knows why we're all being gathered together again?" he asked, mostly to distract himself from his own thoughts. "Is he doing the gathering? Is JB? Is E? Mr. Reardon had all the kids' new addresses in Liston and Clarksville and Upper Tyson—was *he* the one who wanted to force poor Daniella McCarthy to live on Robin's Egg Lane?"

"I don't know," Katherine asked, fiddling with a strand of her hair. "I'm not even sure Mr. Reardon knew about the survivors list."

"It was on his desk," Jonah said.

"But JB put it there," Katherine said. "Not Mr. Reardon. Maybe he was just worried about us seeing the witnesses list."

Jonah jerked his toothbrush back and forth across his teeth with unusual force. He spit again.

"Katherine, it's all a big mystery, okay?" he said. "Maybe we'll never find out all the answers."

"Or maybe we should figure out as much as we can now, so all the final pieces will fall into place at the conference," Katherine retorted.

Jonah frowned at Katherine's reflection in the bathroom mirror. The concentration in her gaze made her look like Sherlock Holmes about to solve his biggest case.

Meanwhile, the toothpaste on his lips made it look like he was foaming at the mouth.

Who's the crazy one? Jonah wondered. *Her or me?*

For his part, Chip kept finding excuses to ride past 1873 Robin's Egg Lane. The house there stayed closed-up and empty.

Chip also tried talking his parents into attending the conference. Embarrassingly, Jonah heard one of his attempts, because Jonah had just stepped onto the Winstons' front porch, ready to ring the doorbell and ask Chip over to play basketball.

"For the last time, no!" a man's voice shouted from inside the house. "I've got a golf date that morning, and your mother's got a spa appointment. We don't have six hours to waste on some namby-pamby, touchy-feely types, who are just going to try to make us feel guilty for not being the perfect parents! Subject closed!"

Jonah stabbed the doorbell.

"You can go with us," he told Chip, as soon as he opened the door. "I'll make my parents take you."

Chip just nodded.

October 28 dawned clear and crisp, the perfect autumn day. Jonah woke up earlier than he usually did on a Saturday, probably because Katherine was already up and banging around in the bathroom. He heard her turning the water on and off, switching the fan from low to high, jerking her towel off the towel rack in a way that rattled the rack against the tile of the wall. He stumbled out into the hall.

"Today's the day!" Katherine announced brightly, as she dodged him to head back to her room, her hair wrapped in a towel.

"Let's go, team," Jonah muttered under his breath,

because the tone of Katherine's words made them sound like they should be accompanied by cartwheels and splits and arms thrown victoriously up in the air.

"Ah, jeez," he whispered, leaning against the bathroom sink. "She really is a cheerleader." And it seemed suddenly that this was true—not because she was an airhead or a hottie or a nonjock, but because she could throw herself so wholeheartedly into someone else's cause, because she could care so much and try so hard from the sidelines.

How could he understand so much about his sister's identity and so little about his own?

Three hours later the whole family—plus Chip—were all loaded into their minivan, headed toward Clarksville Valley High School.

"The weather's so nice, it looks like they'll be able to do some of your sessions outdoors," Mom said, turning around to talk to Katherine, in the middle seat, and Jonah and Chip, in the far back.

"Yeah, I'm really looking forward to the hike and outdoor confidence-building exercises," Katherine said.

A baffled look spread over Mom's face once again.

"Katherine, those teen sessions really aren't intended for *siblings* of adoptees," she said. "It's not too late to turn around and drop you off at home, or at a friend's house, so you're not a . . . a distraction for Jonah and Chip."

Katherine turned around and raised her eyebrow at Jonah, as if to say, *You have to deal with this one.*

"She won't be a distraction, Mom," Jonah said. "Chip and I want her along. Right, Chip?"

"That's right, Mrs. Skidmore," Chip said.

Mom still looked skeptical, as if she knew something was going on. But she turned around and began reading Dad the directions for getting to the school.

Jonah had never been to Clarksville Valley High School. It was a huge new building backing up to a nature preserve, on the very edge of the city. The street leading up to the school was lined with new subdivisions, with houses in various states of completion.

Dad whistled.

"These neighborhoods are so new, you can almost smell the paint drying, can't you?" he said. "Nice houses, huh?"

"We're not moving!" Jonah shouted up from the back-seat.

Both his parents stared back at him.

"Who said anything about moving?" Mom asked.

"Never mind," Jonah muttered.

Act normal, he reminded himself.

They parked close to the front door of the school and joined a line of parents and kids waiting to register at a table in the lobby.

"What did you do, adopt *triplets?*" the woman in front of them asked when she glanced back.

Katherine glowed at the suggestion that she might be the same age as Jonah and Chip.

"No," Mom said, sounding a little reluctant to explain. "This is our son, Jonah, and his friend Chip, whose parents couldn't come today; and our daughter, Katherine, who's not adopted but wanted to be here to, uh, support her brother."

"Well, isn't that nice," the woman said.

"Mom, can we go sit down while you're registering?" Jonah asked, because he didn't want to hear any more of this conversation. And he could see people already filing into an auditorium. If they could just scout out some of the other kids, see if any of them were the ones named on the survivors list, then they'd have an advantage when they broke up into groups later.

"Okay," Mom said.

"Wait—you should get your name tags first," the woman in front of them said. "Here."

She passed back a stack of blank name tags and markers. Jonah's hand shook as he carefully wrote his name, *Jonah Skidmore.* His name had never looked so strange to him before, so alien, as if it didn't really belong to him.

What if I really am supposed to have some other identity? he wondered. *The identity of a boy who's . . . missing? Or from the future? Would I want to know that or not?*

"Hurry up!" Katherine muttered beside him, jabbing her elbow into his side. "We're going to run out of time!"

Jonah put the cap back on the marker, peeled the backing off the name tag, and slapped it on his chest.

"I'm ready," he said, though he didn't feel ready.

The three of them drifted through the crowd, peering at other kids' name tags. Sam Bentree? Nope. Allison Myers? Nope. Dalton Sullivan?

"There was a Dalton on the list, but the last name and the address and phone number were cut off," Chip whispered excitedly. "That *could* be right."

"Let's see if we can find anyone we're sure about, before we try to talk to Dalton," Katherine said. "We can get back to him at the end."

They headed on into the auditorium. Right inside the door they saw a group of kids who were laughing and talking together, as if they had known each other for years. They wore ripped jeans and dark sweatshirts and glared when Jonah stepped close, trying to read their name tags.

"What are you looking at?" one of the guys jeered.

"Oh!" Katherine giggled flirtatiously. "Sorry. We're just looking for some kids we met online, in an adoption chat room. We know their names, but not what they look like. And"—she glanced around, lowered her voice conspiratorially—"our parents don't know we visit those chat rooms!"

"Only dorks visit chat rooms," one of the girls said, looping her arm around the jeering guy's elbow.

"Um," Jonah said. "Okay. Thanks anyway. We'll leave you alone now."

He pulled Katherine away.

"What are you doing?" he asked. "Trying to get beat up?"

"Oh, please," Katherine said. "We have to have some cover story."

"That girl thought you were hitting on her boyfriend!"

"So what?" Katherine put her hands on her hips and stared defiantly at Jonah.

Jonah's head swam. Didn't Katherine understand anything? What if he hadn't been there to protect her?

Chip tugged on Katherine's arm and Jonah's sweatshirt.

"Come on, you two," Chip said. "Cut that out. Let's keep looking."

But Mom and Dad came through the doorway just then. At the front of the auditorium, a man stepped toward a podium on the stage.

"Take your seats, please," he said into the microphone. "We've got a full slate of activities for the day, and I'm sure you're all eager to get started!"

Everyone began sitting down, even the group of tough-looking kids in the back.

Jonah got a seat right on the aisle, so he could peer over sideways at the kids in the next section of seats. The man at the microphone began talking excitedly about what a great turnout they had, what a great program they had planned, how well the county department of social services worked. . . . Jonah tuned him out. There was a Bryce Johnson in the aisle seat across from him, a Ryan—or was that Bryan?—Crockett one row up. Jonah wondered if he could write those names down, pass them along to Chip and Katherine, and get them to shake their heads yes or no without Mom or Dad's noticing. He felt a little guilty that he'd never studied the survivors list the way they had, that he hadn't made a single phone call to any of the other kids.

Jonah turned his head farther, so he could see the girl behind Ryan/Bryan Crockett. She had long blond hair covering her name tag, but she chose that exact moment to flip the hair over her shoulder.

Her name tag said *Sar*—. She flexed her shoulders, stretching in her seat and revealing the rest of the name tag: *Sarah Puchini*.

Sarah Puchini. Yes!

Jonah remembered that name. It was one Katherine had told him when they were in the driveway, playing basketball. So there was at least one other kid at the conference who'd received the mysterious letters, whose name was on the survivors list, who might want to hear what Jonah, Katherine, and Chip knew—and who might have information to share with them, too.

Jonah turned to Chip beside him.

"Sarah Puchini," he whispered in Chip's ear. "One row back."

Chip's face lit up.

On the other side of Chip, Katherine was already standing up.

"What do you think you're doing?" Jonah muttered.

Katherine looked at him blankly.

"They just said for all the kids to go back out to the lobby, to start our activities," she said. "Weren't you listening?"

"Oh," Jonah mumbled.

Mom leaned over the seats.

"It sounds like you guys will be eating your lunch out there on your hike. So we'll just meet you back here at three, okay?"

"Sure," Jonah said.

Dad raised his hand from his armrest in a miniature

good-bye wave and mouthed something that might have been, "Have fun."

Jonah whirled around, hoping he could catch up with Sarah Puchini in the aisle, but her blond head was already disappearing through the door back out into the lobby.

Jonah joined the stream of kids flowing toward the lobby. Chip and Katherine were right behind him. The three of them rushed through the doors together.

"Where is she?" Chip asked, as the crowd came to a stop near the table where everyone had signed in. Jonah could see a woman quietly closing the door to the auditorium behind them, probably to keep the noisy cluster of kids from interrupting the adults' program.

"Don't know," Jonah said, trying to stand on his tiptoes, to get a better look. There was a blond head right up front near the table. No, wait—was that Sarah over toward the side?

"How many kids do you think are here, altogether?" Chip asked.

"Fifty?" Jonah guessed. "Sixty?"

"Angela said there were thirty-six babies on the plane," Chip whispered. "We only had eighteen names to start with. Nineteen, if you count Dalton without a last name."

Did Chip think they should start interviewing all the kids around them? Jonah could just imagine it: *Gotten any strange mail lately? Ever seen anyone disappear? Know anything about time travel?* He didn't think that would go over very well with the tough-looking crowd they'd already annoyed. Those kids were standing in a clump off to the side—now that he was behind them, Jonah could see that their sweatshirts all had skulls on the back.

Nice.

"All right!" a short enthusiastic man with wiry hair called as he dashed halfway up a stairway behind the registration table. He spun around to face the crowd. "Can everyone see and hear me now?"

Mumbles. "Yeah." "Sure." Someone—Jonah thought it was a kid in the skull group—muttered, "Why would we want to?"

"Great!" the man enthused, ignoring or not hearing the surlier comments. "I'm Grant Hodge, a caseworker at the county department of children's services. There are soooo many of you—which is absolutely wonderful; I'm not complaining at all—but we've decided to break you up into two groups for our activities today. One group will come with me, and the other group will go with Carol Malveaux, over there by the door." He pointed. "Wave at everyone, Carol."

A woman with short dark hair lifted her arm and waved vigorously.

"One of us has got to get in the same group as Sarah Puchini," Chip whispered in Jonah's ear.

"I know," Jonah said grimly.

Mr. Hodge was pulling a list out of a folder.

"When I call your name, come stand behind the table if you're with me, or go over by the door if you're with Carol. Got it?" Mr. Hodge was saying. "I'll call my group first."

"Listen to all the names!" Katherine hissed at Jonah and Chip. "We've got to pay very close attention!"

Jonah missed hearing the first name because of Katherine.

"Shh!" He glared at her.

"Jason Ardul," Mr. Hodge said. "Andrea Crowell."

Katherine grabbed Jonah's arm and squeezed hard as a girl with light brown hair quietly slipped around the table at the front.

Jonah and Chip both nodded and mouthed the words, "I know," at Katherine. Andrea Crowell was a name they all recognized. Jonah stared at the girl, to make sure he'd recognize her later on too. She had her hair pulled back in two braids—the style seemed to suit her, though Katherine would probably say it wasn't very fashionable. Andrea was gazing down at her shoes, as if she was too shy to look out at the rest of the crowd.

"Maria Cutler," Mr. Hodge continued. "Gavin Danes."

Another squeeze from Katherine, this one a surprise. Jonah hadn't remembered any Gavin.

Jonah got eight more squeezes before Mr. Hodge reached the middle of the alphabet. Katherine looked so excited she might burst, like a Miss America contestant waiting to hear her own name called.

"Daniella McCarthy," Mr. Hodge said.

Another squeeze, practically breaking Jonah's wrist this time. Jonah winced, squeezed Katherine's arm back even harder, and glanced around, because Daniella McCarthy was someone he really wanted to see. But no one was shoving her way forward in the crowd. No one was stepping aside to make way for the girl who'd been so upset about moving.

"Daniella McCarthy?" Mr. Hodge called again.

The name hung in the air while everyone looked around. Jonah saw Katherine bite her lip, grimacing. Then, suddenly, decisively, she pulled the name tag off her shirt, and crumpled it in her hand.

The minute it was out of sight, she called out, "Oops, sorry. I'm Daniella." She gave a sheepish wave. "My bad. I wasn't listening."

"Kath—" Jonah started to call after her, to yell, "you can't do that!" but she stamped on his foot as she shoved her way forward. The "Kath—" turned into an "ow!" And then she was too far away from him to say anything. She slipped around the table and sidled up between Andrea Crowell and Michael Kostoff.

"What'd she do that for?" Jonah muttered to Chip.

"Beats me," Chip muttered back.

"If we're all in the same group because of this, and we don't get to talk to all the kids, she is in big trouble!" Jonah fumed.

Sure enough, when Mr. Hodge got down to the end of the alphabet, he finished up with, "And Jonah Skidmore and Chip Winston, you're in my group too. All the rest of you, go with Carol."

Jonah stomped up to the front of the group, while everyone else around him except Chip was pushing back toward Carol. He slid up behind Katherine and hissed in her ear, "You go tell them you're in the wrong group right now, so you can talk to the survivors in Carol's group, or, so help me, I'll, I'll . . ."

He was too mad to think of an adequate threat.

Katherine turned to him with troubled eyes.

"Weren't you listening?" she whispered back. "There isn't anyone from the survivors list in the other group."

Jonah blinked. His fury melted into disbelief.

"What?"

"Mr. Hodge called out every single one of the nineteen

names we know, even Dalton Sullivan, who has to be the Dalton on our list," she whispered. "Jonah, we were being sorted."

The way she said *sorted* brought out goose bumps on Jonah's arms. He forced himself to stay calm, to think back, his brain processing information he'd been too angry to fully take in before. Mr. Hodge had called out Sarah Puchini's name—the blond girl was standing over by Anthony Solbers, a chubby boy with pimples. Haley Rivers was behind the table too and Josh Hart and Denton Price and . . .

"But there are other kids in this group, too," he whispered urgently to Katherine. "It's not just kids from the list."

Somehow that detail seemed very important, something to hold on to. Jonah didn't feel like his brain was working very well at the moment, but he knew he wanted other kids around, nonsurvivors. Ordinary kids who had nothing to do with a strange plane or ghost stories or mysterious letters. It was like he believed those kids could protect him.

"Jonah, we never saw the complete list," Katherine reminded him. "Angela said there were thirty-six babies on the plane. I think Mr. Hodge called out thirty-six names."

Jonah stared at his sister in astonishment. He didn't

want his brain working properly now. He didn't want it to reach the conclusion it was racing toward. He wanted to stay numb and ignorant and safe. Most of all, he wanted to stay safe.

Katherine spoke the words for him, shattering his hopes for ignorance.

"I don't know, I can't be sure, but I think . . . ," she began. Her eyes were huge with worry now. "I think, except for Daniella McCarthy, they have all the babies from the plane back together again. Right here. Right now. They have you."

TWENTY-SIX

"Why?" Jonah whispered. But Jonah knew the answer. He didn't even have to think about it.

Beware! They are coming back to get you.

The words from the letter echoed in his mind, leaving room for nothing else but panic.

"Chip!" he whispered in his friend's ear. "If they say, 'Great news! We got an offer to give out free airplane rides this morning'—don't get on the plane! Do you hear me? Don't get on any freaking plane!"

"Okay . . . ," Chip said, puzzled. He apparently hadn't figured anything out, the way Katherine and Jonah had. He hadn't been able to hear their conversation.

Jonah didn't have time to fill him in. He turned back to Katherine.

"Katherine, you've got to tell them you're not Daniella,"

he said. "Maybe that will stop them. Maybe if they just realize she's still in Michigan or wherever—"

"They'd just put me in the other group," Katherine said. "I'm not leaving you and Chip."

She crossed her arms, stubbornly, and jutted out her lower lip just like she always did anytime she fought with Jonah. But today Jonah loved her for it, loved her for it even as he wondered, *What if something happens to me and Katherine both? That would kill Mom and Dad. . . .*

"Besides, you need me around to figure things out," Katherine argued infuriatingly.

"You're not the only one with a brain," Jonah countered.

"I'm the only one whose brain isn't traumatized," Katherine said, looking at Chip, who just now seemed to be putting everything together. His face had gone pale, and he was mouthing the words, "Plane? Plane? Do you really think—?"

At the front of the group, still several steps up on the staircase, Mr. Hodge clapped his hands together.

"All right, group, let's get started. We're the lucky ones—we get to go outside first, while Carol's group is sitting in a classroom," he said.

"Does that mean we'll get stuck in a classroom this afternoon?" someone asked. It was one of the kids with the skull sweatshirts.

Jonah missed Mr. Hodge's answer, because he was thinking, *Oh, please. An ordinary classroom. With some ordinary dull adult voice droning on, so the greatest danger is that I might fall asleep. . . .*

Jonah knew he was in greater danger than that. He could feel the adrenaline coursing through his system, his whole body on alert. But he didn't know what he was supposed to do with all that adrenaline. He didn't know exactly what the danger was. He didn't really believe they were going to be herded onto an airplane.

But do they need an airplane to send us somewhere—sometime—else? What if it's like what happened to Angela, where we take one step forward and suddenly we're gone?

Katherine jabbed an elbow into his ribs. Jonah realized that he'd begun swinging his head from side to side, his arms tensed, and his fists ready, like someone looking for a fight.

"Don't act so weird," she whispered. "People are starting to stare."

Jonah dropped his fists and forced himself to concentrate on what Mr. Hodge was saying.

"Before I go on, I need to introduce Gary Payne, another caseworker who will be assisting me with your group today," he said. "Gary, come on up here."

A younger man, dressed more casually in a sweatshirt

and jeans, jogged up the stairs to stand by Mr. Hodge. He was barely taller than Mr. Hodge, but he was much bulkier. Jonah could see bulging muscles where Gary had pushed up his sweatshirt sleeves.

Muscles?

"Is that E?" Jonah leaned over and whispered urgently to Katherine and Chip.

Helplessly, they both shrugged. Who could tell?

"On the hike, I'll lead the way, and Gary will bring up the rear, to make sure there aren't any stragglers," Mr. Hodge said, grinning to make it seem like a joke. Like, who would want to lag behind on such a beautiful day, on such a lovely hike?

Mr. Hodge began explaining the point of the hike, something about fitting into nature, finding one's identity through connecting with one's environment.

"For the first part of the hike, I want you to walk in complete silence, to really concentrate on what you're seeing around you," he said. "Then we'll stop and chat about what we've discovered in that silence."

We're not allowed to talk? Jonah thought, his panic spiking again. *Not to each other, not to the other kids?*

"Let's head for the middle of the pack," Katherine whispered. "So Gary and Mr. Hodge can't see us talking."

Oh, that's right. Break the rules. It was strange how much relief Jonah felt, realizing that was possible.

Mr. Hodge jumped down from the stairs and began leading the group through a hallway and out a door at the back of the school. Jonah let about a dozen kids file out ahead of him; he could see them stretched out across the yard in the sunshine, headed for the woods of the nature preserve. It was a cheerful scene, but Jonah got chills watching. It reminded him of something, something from when he was a little kid. . . .

The Pied Piper, he thought. He and Katherine had had a book of fairy tales when they were little. She had loved it, but he had hated it, because of one illustration that frightened him: the one of the Pied Piper leading the children of Hamelin to their doom. In the picture the children were skipping and laughing and dancing to the piper's tune, but Jonah knew what was going to happen to them. He couldn't stand for them to be so happy when they ought to be scared.

Mr. Hodge isn't playing any music, Jonah reminded himself. *He's not magical. He can't force us to do anything we don't want to do.*

And yet Jonah was following him, pushing his way out the door. . . .

"We've got to warn the other kids," Jonah murmured to Chip and Katherine.

Katherine looked startled, but Chip nodded and fell back to talk to the boy behind them.

"I'm Chip Winston," he heard Chip say softly. "I called you a few weeks ago—have you gotten any more strange letters?"

No! That approach would take too long! What if they had only a few more minutes?

Jonah sped up and fell into step with the girl ahead of them. He didn't even take the time to glance at her name tag, to see if she'd been on their survivors list or not.

"You can't trust Mr. Hodge or Gary," he muttered. "Pass it on."

She gave him an *Are you crazy?* look and pointedly did not step forward to talk to anyone else.

Jonah sighed and stepped up to the next kid himself.

"You can't trust Mr. Hodge or Gary," he whispered quickly. "We're in danger. Be careful."

Jonah reached three more kids before he felt a hand on his shoulder, just as they were about to step into the woods. It was Gary, who'd rushed up from the end of the line.

"Didn't you hear the instructions?" he hissed in Jonah's ear. "This is the silent part of the walk. If you can't follow directions, you'll have to stay at the back of the line with me."

So they stood at the edge of the woods while all the other kids filed past. Katherine shot Jonah a white-faced worried look as she walked by, but there was nothing she could do.

Chip didn't even glance in Jonah's direction.

Good, Jonah thought. *Pretend you don't know me. Then they won't be watching you, and you can give out the rest of the warnings. . . .*

He could feel the weight of Gary's hand still on his shoulder, heavier than it should be, holding him in place. Finally the last kid walked past, and Gary let go.

"Okay, your turn," Gary said quietly. "But remember— no more talking!"

How could Jonah talk when Gary was right behind him, watching?

Despairing, Jonah trudged forward. He could see the other kids snaking along the trail ahead of him, going deeper and deeper into the woods. Jonah had managed to talk to only five of them. Even if Chip reached all the others, would they believe him? What could they do, anyhow?

After about a mile, Jonah realized that Mr. Hodge was gathering everyone together at the front of the line.

"Circle up," he called out.

He was standing on a rock now, so they could all see

him. Jonah joined the back of the crowd and tried to inconspicuously angle himself away from Gary, toward Katherine and Chip. Gary didn't try to hold Jonah back, but Jonah could feel his eyes on him.

"Few people know this, but there's a rather extensive cave back here, right off the path," Mr. Hodge was saying. "It's one of the best-kept secrets of Clarksville. It's usually off-limits to the public, but we've received special permission to take all of you in. We'll talk about your identities in the cave."

Did those words sound ominous to anyone else? Jonah looked around, but most of the kids just looked bored and distant, as if this was a particularly dull class at school.

Mr. Hodge bent down, ready to scramble down from the rock, but then he straightened up again.

"Oh, I almost forgot," he said. "There's a really interesting rock formation, right as you enter the cave. I forget the exact scientific explanation, but there's something odd about the composition of the rock, so if you spread your hand out and touch it in the right spot, you can feel one patch of the stone that's about fifteen degrees colder than the rest of the rock. It's very bizarre. I'll show you where to touch as we're going in."

Then he hopped down from the rock and led them

downhill, down a winding offshoot trail toward a crevice behind the rock.

"Touch right here," he instructed the first boy behind him, a gangly kid who kept tripping over his own feet. Mr. Hodge pointed to an outcropping along a towering stone wall. "Spread your fingers out—feel it?"

"Uh, yeah," the boy said, sounding surprised.

"Now, you go on through there, and you can sit on one of the benches at the back of the cave," Mr. Hodge said. "Next?"

Jonah watched a girl repeat the same process. After barely a second with her hand against the wall, she jerked back.

"Ow!"

"Oh, you couldn't have felt it that quickly," Mr. Hodge said. "It doesn't hurt. Here. I'll show you."

He took her hand and pressed it against the rock once more.

"See?" Mr. Hodge said.

"Sure," the girl said, but Jonah had the impression that she was just trying to get away. She followed the gangly boy into the cave.

Jonah watched the next few kids, watched the way Mr. Hodge seemed so determined that each kid touch the rock, that each hand linger on the rock for at least a couple of seconds. It reminded him of something from a movie, a scene he couldn't quite remember. It was a movie he'd watched at school, in science . . . the one about that horrible epidemic maybe? Oh, yeah—when the scientists went into their laboratories, where all the deadly viruses were kept, they'd had to place their hands on a scanner to get in, to prove who they really were.

There couldn't be any dangerous viruses in the cave, could there? Not with it hanging open, the air circulating freely . . .

Jonah saw his mistake.

"Katherine!" He spoke softly, through gritted teeth, because Mr. Hodge was looking back at him, looking at all the kids coming down the hill.

Katherine turned her head—maybe it would just look as if she'd heard an unusual birdcall and was trying to listen more closely.

Jonah pretended to trip, stumbling against Katherine's back.

"That's a hand scanner!" he hissed in her ear. "Like fingerprinting! They're checking our identities, making sure we really are the babies from the plane, I bet. Whatever you do, don't touch that rock! Just pretend."

He watched Mr. Hodge pressing another kid's hand against the rock, forcing the kid's palm flat against the stone.

Jonah changed his mind.

"No," he told Katherine. "Run! Run back to Mom and Dad, tell them we're in danger, tell them to come and save us. . . ."

Katherine shook her head, nervous red spots standing out on her pale face.

"What could I say that they'd believe?" she whispered. "No. I'm staying with you."

Jonah thought about grabbing his sister, holding her back, dragging her away to Mom and Dad and safety. Or just bolting himself. The muscles in the backs of his legs tingled, wanting to take off, all but screaming, *Run!* All the adrenaline in his body seemed to have pooled there. It was like the moment in a basketball game when every cell in his body seemed to know, *Time for your breakaway . . . go! Now!*

But what about all these other kids, the ones he and Chip had never gotten a chance to warn? The ones stepping so trustingly into the cave? The ones marveling so stupidly to Mr. Hodge, "Oh, you're right! It is cold!"? The ones who were actually giggling?

How could he leave them behind?

The kids in front of him kept stepping up to the rock, then into the cave. The kids behind him pressed forward, trapping him and Katherine and Chip between them and the stone wall, the rock, and the cave. Even if Jonah decided to run now, he couldn't.

The girl in front of Jonah moved up to the stone wall—it was Andrea Crowell; Jonah recognized the braids from behind. She pressed her hand firmly against the rock, tilted her head to the side, deliberating. She turned to Mr. Hodge.

"Does it have something to do with oxidation levels?" she asked.

Behind Andrea, Katherine held her hand toward the wall. Only Jonah was in a position to see that she didn't actually touch it, that she kept a millimeter of air between her fingertips and the rock.

She stood like that for a long time, then slipped past Andrea into the cave while Mr. Hodge was explaining to Andrea, "I don't know; I'm not a scientist. I've heard the explanation, and it might be something about—what did you call it? Oxi—oops, hold on there, young lady, did you touch the rock?"

He was talking to Katherine now; he'd seen her trying to slip past.

"She did—she took forever," Jonah complained. "Isn't it my turn now?"

Quickly, probably hoping that nobody would notice, Mr. Hodge looked back toward Gary, who was watching from the end of the line. Gary gave a small nod, and Mr. Hodge let Katherine past.

Jonah stepped up to the rock. His knees were trembling now; all the adrenaline seemed to have drained away.

Had he just saved his sister—or doomed her?

TWENTY-SEVEN

They were all in the cave now, lined up on four rows of benches in a surprisingly large, open rock room. One dim lightbulb glowed overhead, casting ghostly shadows on everyone's face. Mr. Hodge had handed off "feel the rock" duties to Gary right after Chip entered the cave, so they hadn't had a chance to whisper to any of the other kids. Jonah was feeling jumpy again. He'd picked the seat closest to the exit, and he had a plan: if anything happened—any strange odor arising out of the deeper part of the cave he couldn't see into, any sound of an airplane, anyone showing up with ray guns or futuristic sunglasses—he'd grab Katherine and Chip and take off running. He'd go for help.

Nothing could happen as long as he sat close to the doorway out. He was sure of it.

From his vantage point, Jonah could see Gary standing by the mysterious spot on the rock wall outside. Gary touched the rock with one finger, then stood there staring, his eyes narrowed, concentrating. Then he touched the rock again, a quick brush of his forefinger. He turned and walked into the cave.

"Is that everyone?" Mr. Hodge asked.

"All good," Gary said, which was a strange answer.

"Very well, then," Mr. Hodge said, smiling.

Gary nodded.

Jonah heard the noise first, a sort of grinding that seemed to be coming from just the other side of the rock wall. Or maybe, *inside* the rock wall. He peered out through the entryway, blinking at the sunshine that filtered down through the trees. And then the sunlight seemed to narrow, to dim.

The entryway was closing.

"No!" Jonah screamed.

He threw himself toward the opening, toward the last rays of sunlight.

The opening was only five steps away, maybe six, and Jonah stretched out his legs, sprinting like he'd never sprinted before. In a second his right foot would be out in the sunlight, he'd slip through—

Something slammed into him from the side, knocking

him to the rock floor. It was like being tackled in football—this was why he'd never liked football—without any pads or helmet. And it was like he was playing on a stone field. And, oh yeah, like his tackler had muscles of stone, as Gary seemed to.

The sunlight disappeared.

"Are you an idiot?" Gary demanded from above him. "You could have been crushed in that door. Killed."

"Caves don't have doors," Jonah muttered back, though his jaw felt broken, smashed against the rock.

"This one does. It's been modified," Gary said. "They want to use it for meetings."

And it was so strange that Jonah and Gary could have that conversation, while behind them, the other kids were gasping and shrieking. Jonah could especially hear Katherine screaming, "Jonah, oh, Jonah, are you okay?"

Oh. She was screaming it directly into his ear, because she was sprawled on the ground beside him.

Gary was scrambling up.

"He's fine," he called out. "He just panicked. I guess we should have warned you that we were closing the door, so we could have some privacy."

"You have to open it," Jonah said, raising his face from the ground. "I—I'm claustrophobic."

He grinned, amazed at his own quick thinking. He

thought maybe he should act a little wacko, so everyone would believe that he'd been freaked out by the notion of being closed in, cut off from the outside world. He stood up. All the other kids were staring at him, their eyes bugging out. . . . Oh. Right. They already thought he was wacko.

"I mean it," Jonah demanded. It was a relief to let all his panic come through in his voice, to sound as scared as he felt. "Open the door. You've got to." His voice cracked. Maybe, on top of everything else, he truly was claustrophobic. The walls seemed closer together than they'd been before. The air seemed to be running out.

"Now, now," Gary said, clamping his hand down on Jonah's shoulder once more. "Calm down. If this is really a problem for you, I can take you out the back entrance, so you don't ruin this workshop for everyone else."

Jonah's eyes met Katherine's. She was still crouched below him. He wanted to ask her advice, work out some plans. If Jonah went off with Gary, could Katherine and Chip and maybe some of the other kids overpower Mr. Hodge? Would they know to do that? Or was Mr. Hodge already too suspicious of Katherine and Chip because he'd seen them with Jonah?

Anyhow, was Gary even telling the truth about a back entrance? All Jonah could picture was himself bound and gagged and hidden at the back of the cave, helpless while all the other kids were taken away.

Jonah took a deep breath, ready to say, "No, that's all right. I feel better now. I can stay." Then suddenly Gary's hand was jerking him backward, pulling him toward the ground again. Jonah's shoulder slammed into the rock, even harder than before.

"What'd you do that for?" Jonah started to ask. But Gary had already let go and was rolling away from Jonah. Jonah raised his head. Now he could see what had happened. Gary hadn't meant to pull Jonah down. Jonah was just collateral damage, falling with Gary when somebody else knocked Gary down. Now Gary and the other man were wrestling on the ground, first one rolling to the top, then the other. The other man was also wearing jeans and a sweatshirt and hiking boots; he was—

"JB!" Katherine shrieked. "You came back!"

Jonah felt the relief flowing through him. He relaxed against the stone floor, letting go of all his fears. JB had protected them before; he'd protect them now. Jonah didn't have to worry about what to do, how to save the other kids. JB would save them all.

Except . . .

JB was getting his head pounded into the stone floor. It'd been quite a while since the last time JB had rolled

over on top of Gary, the last time he'd seemed to be domi-
nating this fight.

Jonah jumped up.

"Katherine!" he screamed. "JB's going to lose if we don't
help him!"

Jonah lunged at the struggling men. He grabbed Gary's
arm—his thick-as-a-tree-stump arm, with biceps as distinct as rope—and, by bracing his feet against the ground,
Jonah managed to keep Gary from punching JB again.

No—scratch that. Gary's arm continued forward. Jonah
had managed only to keep Gary from punching JB quite so
hard.

"Chip!" Jonah screamed. "Help!"

Jonah glanced up to see that Chip and Katherine and
even some of the other kids were rushing toward him.
Katherine, with a girl's sense of fighting, went straight
for the hair, jerking Gary's head back by entwining her
fingers right down to the roots. Jonah had to admit—it
seemed to be working.

Chip and two or three of the other boys were pushing
at Gary's chest, trying to shove him away from JB, while a
few girls tugged JB in the other direction. The other kids
stood by in shock, their faces contorted into masks of dismay and disbelief.

"Is this the role-playing part of the seminar?" he heard

one girl ask hesitantly. "Are we supposed to do something?"

"It's not—" Jonah started to scream at her, but then he decided he didn't have time to explain. "Help us!"

The girl began to crouch down, but it was too late.

Seconds later, Jonah heard the gunshot.

TWENTY-EIGHT

"That's enough," Mr. Hodge said.

He was standing at the front of the room, his right arm in the air, something glistening in his right hand. It didn't look quite like a gun. But Jonah's ringing ears and shattered nerves told him he'd heard gunfire; the adrenaline had come back and was telling him, *That was real! Take cover! Hurry! Before he shoots again!*

Had Mr. Hodge shot straight up into the ceiling? Where had the bullet gone? Where would the next one go? Where would it be safe for Jonah to run?

Gary pulled away from JB, giving Mr. Hodge a chance at a clear shot.

JB only sat up, staring back at him.

"You weren't supposed to bring that into the twenty-first century," JB said. "You know that's illegal."

His voice was calm and resolute, which comforted Jonah somehow. If JB wasn't afraid, then maybe Jonah didn't need quite so much adrenaline coursing through his system.

Then JB's words sank in.

Weren't supposed to bring that into the twenty-first century . . . Was that proof that JB and Gary and Mr. Hodge weren't from the twenty-first century? Jonah wondered. Did that mean that Angela's theory was right?

He still didn't want to believe it.

"Desperate times call for desperate measures," Mr. Hodge was saying with a shrug. "Surely you've heard that one before."

"These are desperate times only because of you," JB retorted.

"*I* didn't choose the century," Mr. Hodge said, taking a step closer to JB and lowering his arm slightly so his gun—or whatever it was—was pointed right at JB. "Children, get away from the interloper. This doesn't concern you."

Before any of the kids had a chance to move, JB reached out and grabbed the girl who'd wondered if the fight was a role-play—*Ming Reynolds* her name tag said. The force of his grasp knocked her name tag from her shirt, and it went fluttering toward the ground, showing the name,

then the blank side, then the name, then the blank side. . . .
JB jerked Ming upright, so they were both standing. He held
her tightly against his chest, like a shield.

"Oh, you wouldn't hurt one of *them*," JB said. "It might
cut into your profits. What are you getting per kid—a
million? Two?"

"That one's only a minor Chinese princess from the
fourth century," Mr. Hodge said, keeping his arm steady.
"Very obscure. Who says I wouldn't sacrifice her to keep
the others?"

"Minor Chinese princess from the fourth century?" What? Jonah
thought. He felt frozen, unable to do anything but watch
JB and Mr. Hodge stare each other down.

"Um, hello? This is seeming a little too realistic. I want
to stop now," Ming said.

JB looked down at the girl, frowned, and carefully set
her to the side.

Jonah immediately stepped between JB and Mr.
Hodge.

"You can't shoot him!" Jonah shouted.

Mr. Hodge began to laugh.

"Amazing," Mr. Hodge said. "And you are . . ." He
squinted at Jonah's name tag. "Jonah Skidmore? So you're
really . . ." Mr. Hodge peered down at the small silver object
in his hand. Jonah wondered if maybe it wasn't a gun, after

all. Maybe it was a Blackberry or a really high-tech, tiny computer with an incredible audio system.

Or maybe his mind was just trying once more to turn something surreal and unbelievable into something ordinary and familiar and easily dismissed.

"Well, that's very interesting," Mr. Hodge muttered.

"What?" Jonah said. He wanted to say, "Who am I?" too. He wanted to understand everything. But the words stuck in his throat.

Mr. Hodge had turned his attention back to JB.

"I can't believe they think you're on their side," Mr. Hodge said. "You must not have told them what you want to do."

"Oh, and you did?" JB taunted.

Mr. Hodge shrugged.

"I'm not the one pretending to have ethics," he said. "*And* I'm taking them to a better place. A better time."

"If the future's still there after we release the ripple," JB said.

Jonah wondered if, on top of developing claustrophobia, he also might have begun to hyperventilate. JB and Mr. Hodge's conversation seemed to be making less and less sense.

"Oh, that's right. I forgot. *You're* allowed to play with time, even if no one else is," Mr. Hodge said.

"We have to protect it," JB said. "You wounded it so badly, we can't follow any of the old rules anymore."

Jonah's head began to throb. He didn't know if it was from being slammed into solid rock so many times, or from the strain of having a gun pointed at him—if it was a gun, or from the effort he was making to come up with an explanation for everything he'd witnessed. But it was getting harder and harder to think straight. He glanced over his shoulder, hoping JB could give him some directions.

JB was gazing past Jonah, past Mr. Hodge, even, into the darkness beyond.

Backup, Jonah thought. Of course. JB wouldn't have planned to overpower Mr. Hodge and Gary all by himself. He would have brought the other janitor from the FBI, the one who'd given Jonah the Mountain Dew. Maybe he'd even brought Mr. Reardon—maybe he was in on this too.

The person who stepped out of the shadows was Angela DuPre.

Gary evidently saw her at the same moment that Jonah did, because he screamed, "Watch out! Behind you!"

Mr. Hodge whirled around, pointing his gun at Angela now, instead of JB. But Angela had a gun too. Or, no—hers looked more like a toy, all black and yellow. Then she pointed it at Mr. Hodge and a stream of light shot across the room, jolting him. Mr. Hodge let out a scream and fell to the ground, twitching. The silver object in his hand hit the ground too and skittered across the floor, toward Jonah.

Jonah reached down and scooped it up. Out of the corner of his eye, he could see JB bending over Mr. Hodge and Angela fiddling with the front part of her gun. And Gary? Where was Gary? Jonah turned his head, and there was Gary racing toward him, ready to slam into him yet again. Jonah took a step back, but it wasn't necessary. Before his second step, Gary was on the floor, screaming and twitching like Mr. Hodge.

"Is that a ray gun?" Jonah asked, in awe, because this, finally, would be proof he couldn't ignore.

"Nope," Angela said. "Just a regular twenty-first-century Taser. I ordered it off the Internet."

"But the lights," Jonah said. "And—"

"That's just the laser tracking system," Angela said. "The electrical charge goes through the barbs."

Jonah saw that JB had looped thin silvery bands around Mr. Hodge's wrists and ankles and was pulling little barbs that looked like fish hooks out of Mr. Hodge's chest. Then he rushed past Jonah to do the same with Gary. Both men had stopped screaming and twitching, but they seemed too dazed to put up much resistance.

"Quick, Angela, get the ropes," JB said. "So we can tie them up firmly."

Angela rushed back toward the dark section of the cave.

"I'm a Boy Scout," Jonah said, turning toward JB. "I can help with that."

Instantly, he felt humiliated for saying that—how nerdy could he be? He didn't have to look back at Katherine to know that she was probably rolling her eyes, mouthing the words, "Really, we're not related. Not by blood."

JB grinned as he straightened up.

"Thanks, Jonah," JB said. "You've been *very* helpful today. You just hand me that Elucidator, and then we'll let you tie some knots."

He had his hand outstretched, his fingers so close to the object in Jonah's hand that he easily could have grabbed it. But he was clearly expecting Jonah to pass it over without any problem. He waited patiently.

"This thing?" Jonah said, pulling back a little. He looked down at the object, which seemed more like a remote control to him now. "This is an Elucidator? What's that mean?"

"It means it's not something you want to mess with," JB said. "It's very dangerous."

Jonah remembered Mr. Hodge looking at it, muttering

about Jonah's identity. *So you're really . . . Well, that's very interesting. . . .*

"This 'Elucidator' is from the future, isn't it?" Jonah asked, holding it even more tightly.

JB hesitated.

"Yes," he finally said.

Jonah took a step back. JB still stood there waiting, but he was squinting now, getting anxious. Beyond JB, Jonah could see all the other kids watching him, wondering what he was going to do. Moments before, some of the kids had been shrieking as loudly as Mr. Hodge and Gary, but now they, too, had gone silent. It seemed like they were all holding their breath.

"Jonah," JB said. "Give me the Elucidator. Now."

Jonah raised the Elucidator, but only to point it at JB.

"No," he said.

TWENTY-NINE

"Angela!" JB called. "The Taser!"

Instantly, Jonah saw his mistake. In a second, Angela would turn around and aim her Taser at him, and they'd just re-enact the scene from a few moments ago. Except this time it would be Jonah writhing on the floor and then passing out, and JB scooping up the fallen Elucidator. And then . . . what would happen then?

Jonah didn't know, but he could still hear Mr. Hodge's words echoing in his brain: *I can't believe they think you're on their side. You must not have told them what you want to do.* What did that mean? What should Jonah do? Was there anyone he was sure he could trust?

That was one question he could answer.

"Katherine!" he called out. "Catch!"

He tossed the Elucidator in the air, an easy toss, easier

than passing a basketball. He knew without turning to look that Katherine would catch it, that she would hold on tightly, that she wouldn't betray him. She might make fun of him, she might roll her eyes and call him an idiot, but she wouldn't let go. She'd already proved that.

As soon as the Elucidator was in the air, Jonah took off running. JB made no attempt to stop him because he was spinning around, following the arc of the Elucidator. So Jonah had a clean, fast sprint to the back of the cave. He needed the speed; he needed the element of surprise if he had any prayer of wrestling the Taser out of Angela's hand before she aimed it at him.

He was too late.

Even in the dimness of the back of the cave, Jonah could see that Angela had already turned around. In one smooth quick move, she pulled a cartridge from her pocket, reloaded the Taser, and pointed it back toward Jonah.

Jonah took a stumbling step to the side, just in case he had a chance of dodging the laser light and the barbs and whatever else the Taser was about to send zinging at him. He hoped it wouldn't hurt too badly. He hoped he wouldn't scream as loudly as Gary and Mr. Hodge had. He hoped . . .

Angela held the Taser steady, aiming past Jonah. Aiming toward Mr. Hodge and Gary.

"Shoot Jonah!" JB was yelling helpfully.

Thanks a lot, Jonah thought. He didn't have any hope now. He was too close to Angela, too close to reverse his course, too close for her to miss. Just as soon as she corrected her aim and squeezed the trigger, he'd be on the ground.

Angela spun toward Jonah, but she didn't squeeze the trigger. She stepped forward and glanced out toward the brighter part of the cave, though that made no sense— surely Jonah was blocking her view. She turned the Taser sideways, not pointing at anyone anymore. Then she reached over and slid the Taser into Jonah's grasp.

She was handing over her weapon.

"What?" Jonah demanded, dumfounded.

Angela pressed a finger to her lips, then she moved the finger and began to scream.

"No! You can't have it!"

Jonah's ears were reverberating with all that lung power released in such a small space. But already Angela was expecting him to listen. She leaned in close and whispered in his ear, "I really am on your side. Completely. You deserve to know the truth. So pretend that you captured me."

Jonah just stood there. He was so stunned he almost dropped the Taser.

"Maybe you should shout something about getting the ropes?" Angela whispered, bending down to pick up looped coils from the floor of the cave.

"Move it! Get those ropes now!" Jonah hollered. His voice cracked; surely that wasn't a convincing yell.

But Jonah could hear JB calling from the lighter part of the cave, "Angela! What happened?" before breaking off to warn Katherine, "Young lady! Really—you can't press any of those buttons! You don't know what they do!"

"What's going on?" Jonah hissed at Angela. "Tell me!" She grimaced.

"There isn't time to talk. Besides, you should hear it from the experts, not me." She nudged him. "Go on."

Jonah started to back out of the darkness.

"A-hem," Angela said. She stepped in front of him and moved her hand over his so that the end of the Taser was pressed into her ribcage. "Don't you dare set that off now—you're too close," she whispered. "But *please*, make it look like it's possible that you captured me."

"Angela?" JB called again, sounding even more worried.

Angela dropped her hand from the Taser. Together, Jonah and Angela stepped out into the light.

"He got your weapon?" JB said incredulously. "He overpowered you?"

"He's a very strong young man," Angela said defensively. "Stronger than he looks."

Well, that was an insult, wasn't it? Jonah dug the Taser more deeply into Angela's ribs. He shoved her forward, more roughly than he'd intended.

"Maybe not quite so realistic," she muttered.

"Give the ropes to Chip," Jonah ordered.

"Uh, Jonah, I'm not a Boy Scout," Chip said. "My dad said he didn't have time for all those camp-outs, so I don't know anything about tying knots, and—"

"Here," Jonah said, slapping the Taser into Chip's hand. "Shoot her if you have to."

Anguish spread over Angela's face. Jonah could tell she wasn't acting now, either, because it was Chip holding the Taser, and there was no way Jonah could signal Chip to let him know that she was really on their side, without JB's seeing as well.

Jonah tied Mr. Hodge's and Gary's wrists and ankles. They lay calmly now, their eyes half-closed. Jonah couldn't tell if they were still dazed, or if they were faking it, biding their time. He tied the knots as quickly as he could.

He walked toward JB, ropes still dangling from his hands.

"Not me, too?" JB asked, with an ingratiating grin. "I think you've gotten confused. Remember—I was the one trying to save all of you."

"What were you saving us from?" Jonah asked in a dull voice. "What were you saving us for?"

"Tell your sister to give me the Elucidator, and I'll explain," JB said.

"Explain, and maybe we'll decide that you deserve the Elucidator," Jonah said.

He looped the rope around JB's wrists and tied his firmest knot yet. JB didn't resist. Then Jonah tied JB's ankles and Angela's ankles and wrists.

Someone was sniffling behind him.

"Oh, please." It was Ming, the girl who'd temporarily been a human shield. "Just open the door and let us go to our parents. My cell phone isn't working—I've been trying and trying to call the police—once we're out of the cave, I'm sure it will work right. . . ."

Jonah hadn't even thought about cell phones, but now he noticed that just about every kid had one out. One boy near the back bench kept stabbing a finger at his phone three times, waiting, stabbing three times again, waiting. . . .

Nine-one-one, Jonah thought. *Of course.* His knees almost gave way at the thought that a bunch of police officers in dark uniforms would soon come swarming into the cave, saving them all, saving Jonah from having to make any more choices, any more mistakes.

Then Jonah realized that the reason the boy kept stabbing at the phone was that none of his calls was going through.

"Sure," he told Ming. "You find a way to open that door; we're all out of here."

"No! Don't!" JB shouted.

"Oh, let them try," Gary said groggily from the ground. "There's a keypad by the entryway. The code is twenty-one ST."

Was it a trick?

Jonah turned back to JB.

"What will happen if we try that code? If we open the door?" he demanded.

"You'll see. . . . You'll find out too much, all at once," JB said. "It might scare you."

"It might scare you"? After everything that's already happened, JB's worried about scaring us?

Jonah decided to take his chances.

He rushed toward the entryway, and it was as if *he'd* become the Pied Piper now. Most of the other kids shoved in behind him. His finger shook as he pressed in 2 1 and then ST. An image was growing in his mind of what he might see when the door slid back. Maybe, somehow, Gary and Mr. Hodge had already slipped them into the future. They'd step out of the cave, and all the trees would

be gone; the newly built houses would be ancient and falling down. That *would* be scary, but Jonah was braced for it.

The door began moving, slowly this time, like it was
an ancient boulder covered with a thousand years of moss.
As soon as there was a crack between the door and the
wall, Jonah darted toward it, peeking out. He peeked out
and saw . . .

Nothing.

THIRTY

Behind him, other kids began to scream in terror, but Jonah could only stare. It wasn't dark beyond the cave door—darkness would be *something*; darkness would mean that, with a little light, there'd be plenty to see. Darkness would be comforting, actually. This was so much worse. There was just enough light filtering out from the cave to show that there were no trees anymore, no houses, no path, no rocks, no clouds, no sky. Nothing. It was like being deep in outer space, so far away from everything else that he couldn't even see any stars.

"We're in a black hole!" someone screamed behind him.

Automatically, instinctively, Jonah hit the keypad again: 2 1 ST. He hoped it was like the garage-door opener at home, where the same code worked for opening and closing. Mercifully, the door began to roll shut again.

"It's not a black hole," another kid was explaining, sounding perfectly rational. "In a black hole the gravity would crush us."

"It reminds me of the Bible," a girl said thoughtfully. "Genesis. 'The Earth was without form and void. . . .'"

Jonah grabbed the "not a black hole" boy and the girl who'd thought of the Bible and pulled them through the crowd. He wanted people by his side who could think when everyone else was screaming. He walked back to the adults, who were all sitting on the floor now, with their backs against the wall, Chip and Katherine pointing the Taser and the Elucidator at them. Gary and Mr. Hodge looked amused. JB and Angela looked distressed.

"Explain," Jonah demanded. "Where are we?"

"The more appropriate question," Mr. Hodge said teasingly, "would be, 'When are we?'"

JB kicked at him, with both legs at once, since JB's legs were tied together.

"Don't be cruel," JB said. "This is bound to be very traumatic for all of them." He looked over at the screaming, hysterical mass of kids clustered by the door, then back at Jonah. "We call this a time hollow. When they shut the door, Hodge and Gary pulled this whole cave outside of time."

"So, what—like, we don't exist right now?" the "not a black hole" kid asked. Jonah glanced at him more closely now. He had curly blond hair, kind of like Chip's. His name tag said *Alex*.

"No," JB said. "We exist. But 'now' doesn't."

"Why not?" the girl said. Her name tag said *Emily*.

JB glanced toward the hysterical crowd once more.

"Get them calmed down," he said. "And make them sit on the benches again. Hodge and Gary and I will explain everything."

"We will?" Gary growled.

"*I* will," JB said. "And it's fine with me if they hear only my version."

"We'll explain too," Hodge muttered.

It took forever to get all the kids back to the benches, to get them to be quiet. Jonah thought he and Emily and Alex had accomplished it when one kid happened to glance at his cell phone.

"It still says ten eighteen!" he screamed. "It's said ten eighteen since we got here!"

"Shh, shh," Emily soothed him. "Sometimes cell phones break."

She sat beside him, holding his hand, and that seemed to calm him down.

Katherine, Chip, and a few other kids had worked to

pull the adults to the front of the room. They stood like dangerous prisoners on trial, Katherine and Chip guarding them from the side.

"Just show them the presentation," Hodge was suggesting.

"You mean, your commercial?" JB sneered. "No way."

"You can give the counterpoint afterward," Gary said. "We promise."

"Let them," Angela said. "You showed it to me."

JB frowned, then shrugged.

"All right," he said.

"Go into demo mode on that Elucidator, sugar," Hodge told Katherine. "See the DEMO button at the top?"

Katherine glared, offended by the "sugar." But she seemed to be following his orders.

"Let me guess," she said. "The one that says ADOPTION PROMO?"

"You got it," Hodge said. "Now aim at the wall."

Instantly, on the front wall of the cave, a movie screen appeared. No—Jonah went over and touched it—it was still solid rock. No light shone from the Elucidator, but it was clearly the source of both the screen and the images that suddenly glowed from the screen: shifting photographs of hundreds of faces, seeming to represent every era and culture in history. Despite the rock surface, the

faces were clear and unruffled. This was beyond high defi-
nition; it was like watching reality.

"From the time humankind achieved time travel," a
voice boomed out, just like in a movie preview, "people
have been stirred with compassion for the sufferings of
the past."

What followed was a montage of images that Jonah
could barely stand to watch. People lost their heads to guil-
lotines; soldiers on horseback ran swords through infants,
bodies fell into pits dug to bury the living with the dead.
It went on and on and on, agonizingly. Jonah felt like he'd
seen all the worst moments of human history by the time
the killings finally ended.

"I'm not allowed to watch R-rated movies!" a kid behind
Jonah screamed. "Make it stop!"

"Shh. It's over now," a girl's voice comforted. "It's in the
past." Jonah looked back—it was Emily again.

On the screen now, all the death and destruction was
replaced by a grim-faced man sitting in what appeared to
be a TV studio. A caption at the bottom of the screen
identified him as Curtis Rathbone, CEO, Interchronological Rescue.

"The past was a very brutal place," he intoned solemnly.
"But as much as modern humanity's hearts went out to their
ancestors, their antecedents, they knew that the paradox

and the ripple would make intervention very difficult."

"Pause it for a moment, will you?" JB called out. "I think you need a few definitions."

Katherine squinted at the Elucidator. "Where is—oh, wait, wait, I got it!"

Curtis Rathbone, CEO, froze on the screen.

"The *paradox*," JB called out. "That's the possibility that time travelers might cause some event in the past that would lead to their own nonexistence. Such as, for instance, accidentally killing their own parents. And the *ripple* is what we call any significant change caused by time travelers, which then alters the present and the future. Think of a stone thrown into a pond, and the way the ripples spread out to the very edge of the water. . . . Is that clear? Does everyone understand?"

Jonah expected the other kids to begin shouting out, "Time travel? What are you talking about? Are you nuts?" or "The ripple? The paradox? Yeah, right. Try the psych ward!" But when he looked around, the faces around him were as solemn as Curtis Rathbone's. The other kids had seen the nothingness outside their cave; they were ready for explanations, however far-fetched.

"Okay, back to the propaganda," JB said.

On the screen, Curtis Rathbone began talking again.

"We here at Interchronological Rescue were determined

to take action," he said. "We studied time very carefully, centuries worth of wars and genocide, famines and pestilence—all the very worst of human suffering. And we discovered hundreds whose deaths were so horrendous, so chaotic, so terrible, we knew we had to save them. And we knew we *could*."

Someone gasped behind Jonah.

"That's right," Curtis Rathbone said, almost as if he'd heard the gasp. "Rescue was possible. Oh, we knew we couldn't save everyone. Much as we would have liked to, say, save every victim of the twentieth-century European Holocaust, we knew that was off-limits. The ripple would have been extreme—too much happened as a result of that Holocaust. But to save even the small, insignificant victims of the past—the 'orphans of history,' as it were—didn't our own humanity demand that we try?"

A single tear glistened in Curtis Rathbone's eye. He dabbed at it and smiled fleetingly out from the screen.

"We began ten years ago, rescuing children of the Spanish Inquisition," he said. "Babies left in houses that were then burned to the ground, children left for dead who were easily revived by our modern techniques—we could save them! Save them without causing a ripple or a paradox, because they had as good as vanished from history, even without our intervention. And, thus, we could transform those dark days of humanity into a triumph of the human spirit, of modern humanitarianism." Now he beamed out at the crowd, the terrors of history receding into the past.

"The response of the modern age has been overwhelming," Rathbone continued. "Everyone was eager to adopt a desperate child from the past, to reach out across the centuries to save some poor soul who had never had a chance. Within five years, we were running ten rescue missions a week, in every century since the beginning of time. Our generous age paid for plastic surgery for Neanderthals, counseling for war refugees, reconstructive surgery for land-mine victims. . . . And then we perfected our age reversal techniques, so the children we rescued didn't even have to remember their ordeals. We could deliver perfect happy, healthy bouncing babies to our clients—"

"That's enough!" JB snarled. "Turn it off!"

Katherine must have managed to hit the right buttons, because Curtis Rathbone disappeared from sight. Maybe it was Jonah's imagination, but the lights in the room seemed a bit brighter as well.

"Perhaps Curtis Rathbone had humanitarian intentions in the beginning," JB growled. "Perhaps."

"He did!" Hodge shouted. "He does!"

JB ignored him.

"But what Interchronological Rescue became was something entirely different," he said bitterly. "Purveyors of prestigious names from history for wealthy idiots who want to brag at their cocktail parties, 'Oh, yes, my little Henry comes from a line of British kings.' . . . Didn't you try to kidnap Amelia Earhart out of the skies over the Pacific? Didn't you lure Ambrose Bierce to the Mexican border?"

"The age reversal doesn't work on adults," Gary muttered.

"You know that—now," JB countered.

"Hold on," Jonah said, because no one else was speaking up. "Age reversal?"

JB flashed him an angry glance, then turned his glare back to Hodge.

"Traumatized children from traumatic times in history have a lot of issues," JB said sarcastically. "There were problems Interchronological Rescues never wanted to talk about, never wanted the prospective adoptive parents to know about."

"Erase the memories and you erase the problems," Hodge said cheerily. "What's wrong with that?"

Jonah stared at Hodge, trying to understand.

"This is one of the few parts of the theory I was right about," Angela spoke up, apologetically. "They had turned you all into babies again, even though some of you had once been much older. Teenagers, even."

Angela's words seemed to echo in the stone room. *Turned you all into babies again* . . . Watching JB's outrage, Jonah had almost forgotten that any of this time-travel talk had anything to do with him.

"Us?" he whispered. "You're talking about us?"

JB was still glaring at Hodge and Gary.

"Interchronological Rescue got sloppy," he accused. "They began taking children whose disappearances were noticed. They caused ripple upon ripple upon ripple. . . ."

He closed his eyes, pained beyond words.

"Oh, and your intervention worked so well," Hodge accused. "We could have repaired the ripples. We could have put a few children back, if we had to. But, no, you and your friends insisted on attacking, right in the middle of the time stream—"

"The time crash was not my fault!" JB screamed. "If you'd just surrendered . . . You're the one who chose to speed away, to slam into the time frame, to ruin her life"—he pointed at Angela—"to nearly destroy thirteen years of time—no, to nearly destroy all of time!"

Even tied up, they were about to come to blows again. Jonah had had it. He'd had it with the suspense, the implications, the accusations, the strain. He stood up. That wasn't enough. He climbed up on top of a bench and yelled, "Who are we?"

JB and Hodge both fell silent. Then JB said, "Show them. They're going to have to find out eventually."

"It's F six on the Elucidator," Hodge said.

Jonah watched his sister hit a button. The screen reappeared, displaying a chart. It was a seating chart, Jonah realized, like for a classroom. Or an airplane. He stepped down from the bench to get a closer look and squinted at the names: Seat 1A, Virginia Dare

1B, Edward V of England

1C Richard of Shrewsbury

His eyes skimmed down the list, looking for boys' names, or names that sounded familiar: 9B, John Hudson; 10C, Henry Fountain; 11A, Anastasia Romanov; 12B, Alexis Romanov; 12C, Charles Lindbergh III. . . .

"That's who you are," JB said quietly. "You're the missing children of history."

THIRTY-ONE

"Which one am I?" Jonah demanded. But his voice got lost in the sea of voices around him, all calling out the same question. And shouting, "How could it be?" "That's not possible!" "I can't believe it!"

"Believe it," JB said, his voice carrying over the shouts. "It's true."

Incredibly, Mr. Hodge was nodding too.

"Virginia Dare," he said. "First child born of English parents in the Americas. Who vanished with the rest of Roanoke Colony. Edward and Richard, the British princes who vanished from the Tower of London in 1483. Anastasia and Alexis, the two youngest children of Czar Nicholas II, who disappeared during the Russian Revolution. The kidnapped Lindbergh baby, the so-called Eaglet . . . It was my best rescue mission ever."

"It was your worst rescue mission ever!" JB retorted. "If we hadn't discovered how to hold back the ripple, just temporarily, just until we can heal all the wounds, until we can return the children to their rightful place in history . . ."

Jonah's head was spinning. He knew he should be paying attention, listening closely. He had the feeling that JB had just said something important, but he couldn't quite grasp what he meant, couldn't quite understand.

"What?" This was Katherine, exploding. "You want to send everyone back in time?"

Oh. That was what JB meant. That was important, all right.

Suddenly the whole room was quiet, everyone stunned into silence at once. Katherine turned the Elucidator away from the wall, aiming it at JB once more.

"You can't do that," she said. "I won't let you."

JB held out his hands apologetically, a particularly pitiful gesture with his wrists bound.

"I'm sorry," he said softly. "I wish there were some other way. It's not fair to any of you. But . . . some of you are royalty. Or the children of explorers. You can understand the need to sacrifice for your country, to take risks for all of humankind. This is even more important. Yes, returning you to history may be dangerous for many of you. Even deadly. But—think of it as your chance to save the world.

To give your own life in order to help every other person on the planet, for all time."

Someone began clapping. It was Mr. Hodge.

"Oh, very noble," he said sarcastically, his clapping too slow and exaggerated to be sincere. "What a pretty speech. But you forget, my friend, that these children haven't been raised as royalty. Or as sacrificial lambs. They think of themselves as twenty-first-century Americans. They're selfish. Spoiled. Overprivileged. The richest society in history, up to this point. They aren't capable of sacrifice."

Jonah waited for some kid to speak out, to complain, "We're not selfish!" But nobody said a word. They were all watching Mr. Hodge.

"What *I'm* offering—myself and Gary, that is—is the glorious future," he said. "Even more privilege than you've ever imagined. Technology beyond your wildest dreams. I mean, we have *time* travel—you can be sure that the video games will be truly awesome!" His eyes seemed to twinkle hypnotically. "I just want to complete my original mission. That ripple effect he's so worried about"—he pointed at JB jeeringly—"pah! You won't even feel it!"

He took a hop-step toward Katherine; he seemed barely constrained by the ropes around his ankles.

"We've worked so hard to bring you all together again,"

he said softly now. "The time crash put thirteen years off-limits, but we came back for you as soon as we could. Just hand me that Elucidator, sweetie, and we can all be on our way. There are families waiting for you!"

Katherine jerked the Elucidator back, away from Mr. Hodge.

"All the kids here already have families," she said coldly. She stared defiantly toward Jonah, as if she expected him to spring to her side, to link arms and agree: "Yeah! What she said!"

He didn't move.

"And, if we do what you want, we'd have to go back to being babies again?" a voice said quietly from the crowd. Jonah looked back—it was Andrea Crowell, the girl with braids. "We'd have to forget everything, forget our entire lives? Forget everyone we've ever known?"

"Well, uh, yes, but it's not like you'd even remember that you'd forgotten anything," Mr. Hodge said, looking uncomfortable. "You'll be perfectly happy in the future. I promise."

Jonah looked from Mr. Hodge to JB. Both of them were staring back at him as if they expected him to make some sort of decision. He glanced back over his shoulder—several of the other kids were peering anxiously toward him as well. Why?

Oh, yeah, Jonah thought. *I did kind of take charge before. Grabbing the Elucidator, "capturing" Angela, opening the door, closing the door* . . . He felt like climbing up on top of the bench again and calling out, "Hey, guess what? I'm good at quick things—snap decisions, rash actions—that's all. This one's too big for me. Someone would have to think about this one for a long, long time. That's not my department."

But no one else was talking.

Jonah sighed.

"What if we just want to stay in our own time?" he asked. "This is where we belong—the twenty-first century, I mean."

"But the future's even better," Mr. Hodge said, as JB interjected, "No, you really *don't* belong in the twenty-first century."

"Yes, we do," Jonah said stubbornly.

JB shook his head.

"It was just a mistake, all of you ending up where you did. *When* you did," he said. "Hodge was carrying his load of stolen babies to the future, and we—those of us who enforce the laws of time travel—we knew we had to stop him as soon as we could. There's a protocol to stopping in the middle of the time stream, steps everyone agrees to, to avoid doing even more damage. Hodge broke every rule."

"Oh, come now, that's impossible," Hodge said mockingly. "You time fanatics have so many rules, it'd take an eternity to break them all."

JB glared at Hodge. Jonah could hear a few kids in the back of the room snickering.

"I'm not explaining this well enough," JB said, looking back at Jonah. "It's really complicated, but I'll try to put this in terms you can understand. It'd be like a criminal kidnapping a bunch of babies in New York City and trying to fly them to Los Angeles. But when he's caught in the middle of the country, he refuses to give up. Instead he crash-lands in Kansas City and sets off a nuclear weapon that completely destroys the Midwest." He paused, looking down at the ropes around his wrists. Then he peered up again, earnestly. "I'm trying to undo that nuclear explosion."

Everyone was silent for a long moment. Then Katherine complained, "That's a stupid comparison. A nuclear explosion in Kansas City would kill all the stolen babies, too."

Other kids began muttering as well—Jonah heard Alex say, "But the nuclear fallout blowing toward Los Angeles would be kind of like that time-ripple thing he was talking about. . . ."

Jonah held up his hand and, to his amazement, everyone stopped talking.

"Okay, I get it that nobody planned for us to end up here," he said. "But that's what happened, and so we've lived all our lives in the twentieth and twenty-first centuries, and so this *is* where we belong now. It's what we know. It's where our families are."

His eyes skimmed over Katherine's face as he said that. She smiled encouragingly.

"Look." Jonah peered at Mr. Hodge. "You're just going to have to find some other babies for those families in the future. And you—" he turned his attention to JB. "You're going to have to figure out some other way to fix the ripple, to save time. I'm sure you can think of something. I don't know about the other kids, but I'm staying here!" This would have come off very well, very dramatically, except that he realized he wasn't saying exactly the right thing and was forced to add, weakly, "I mean, I'm staying *now*. Whatever. You know what I mean."

Mr. Hodge smiled. Slyly.

"That's what I've always loved about twenty-first-century Americans," he said. "They're always so convinced that they can control their own destinies. Go on, then. Walk out that door. Have a nice life."

And then Jonah remembered the nothingness on the other side of the door, the fact that the twenty-first century—and everything else outside the cave—had disappeared.

"Tell me the code to go home," he said. "Please."

Mr. Hodge shook his head. Jonah turned to JB. After a second's hesitation, JB began shaking his head too.

"You're going to have to choose," he said. "Your 'now' is off-limits. Which will it be—the future or the past?"

THIRTY-TWO

Nobody got hungry. Nobody had to go to the bathroom. Those were the good things. But, also, nobody could leave the cave. Nobody could go back to their regular lives, see their parents again, talk to their usual friends. Grow up.

Before, Jonah had had no sense of time stopping. He'd been too busy crashing to the floor, grabbing for the Elucidator, running for the ropes. But now, time—or really the lack of it—hung heavily on him. He didn't even care anymore about finding out which missing child from history he actually was. The other kids were no more motivated. Everyone sat around, completely enervated.

"You know that saying about how time flies when you're having fun?" Emily, the girl who'd been so soothing before, asked as she plucked pointlessly at her sweatshirt sleeve.

"Yeah," Jonah said.

"I thought the opposite of that was the last five minutes of math class, when the teacher's going on and on and on about decimals," she said. She yawned. "I didn't know it could be *this* bad."

"Yeah," Jonah said again. He thought about adding, "I know what you mean," but it didn't seem to be worth the effort.

Think, he commanded himself in disgust. *Make a decision. Future or past? Past or future?*

He couldn't decide. It was like taking one of those multiple-choice tests in school when he wasn't sure of the answer, so he tried eliminating all the choices he was sure were wrong—and then discovered that there were no possible right answers left. Going to the future would mean giving up everything. For that matter, so would going to the past.

And probably dying, on top of everything else. He couldn't get the images out of his head of all those brutal deaths from history: the chopped-off heads, the swords slicing flesh, the hail of gunfire raining down on children.

"I'm a coward," he whispered to himself. "I don't want to die. Especially not like that."

But he'd been raised by such nerdy, square parents, who'd dragged him off to Sunday school and Boy Scout meetings, and had talked so seriously about how important it was to be a good person. Because of that, he kind of felt like JB had the best argument. JB wanted to save the world.

Mr. Hodge and Gary didn't seem to care.

"I don't want to die," he muttered, a little more loudly this time.

Maybe if everyone agreed to go back to the past, he'd be one of the lucky ones. Maybe he'd be someone who just kind of accidentally vanished from history, who still had a good life waiting for him in the past. Maybe he was one of those British princes. He could get used to chomping down on a huge turkey leg like some old-time king in a movie, couldn't he? And living in a castle, and having thousands of soldiers at his command, and . . .

He looked around. He didn't want any of the other kids to die either.

Angela caught his eye. Cautiously, as if she was trying not to be seen by anyone else, she raised one eyebrow and mouthed something—"Walk"? What did that mean? Oh. No. Maybe it was "Talk"?

What good was that? How could they talk when she was still sitting right next to JB?

Jonah remembered Katherine was still holding the Elucidator. Chip still had the Taser in his hand. They still had some control.

Jonah stood up.

"We're facing a very important choice," he said. *Wonderful*, he thought. *I sound like someone running for seventh-grade student council.* But everyone was staring at him now. He had to go on. "And yet, we don't know if we can trust the information we've been given." He turned to face the adults. "How do we know you're not all working together?"

JB and Mr. Hodge looked at him like he'd gone crazy. It was kind of a no-brainer—Jonah was absolutely certain that those two weren't on the same side. Still, Jonah forged ahead.

"So we're going to take each of you to a different corner of the room and talk to you individually," he said.

"What good will that do?" one of the other kids jeered.

It figured—it was one of the kids in black sweatshirts with the skulls on the backs.

Jonah shrugged.

"I think it's worth a try," he said. "It's better than sitting around doing nothing."

Somehow, that energized the other kids. Within five minutes—or, what would have been five minutes, if time had been moving—one group of kids was clustered around Gary in the front right part of the cave and another around Mr. Hodge in the front left. Chip was with JB and a few others in the back right corner; and Jonah, Katherine, Alex, and Emily were in the group with Angela in the back left.

"Quick—what do you think we should do?" Jonah hissed.

One look at Angela's anguished face killed his hopes.

"I don't know much more about this time-travel stuff than you do," she said. "I can tell you this—the man you keep calling JB is sincere. That Hodge character doesn't seem very trustworthy."

Great. Jonah had managed to figure that out all by himself.

"What's JB's real name?" Katherine asked.

"Names in the future are very weird," Angela said. "I can hardly pronounce it—it's something like Alonzo Alfred Aloysius K'Tah—you might as well keep calling him JB."

"How far in the future are we talking about?" Emily asked.

"He won't tell me," Angela said. "He says I've already been contaminated enough." She grinned. "He says I was supposed to marry a plumber and have five kids. I told him, 'Uh-uh, I don't think so!' He must have had me mixed up with somebody else."

Jonah closed his eyes for a moment. Maybe JB and Hodge and Gary had *Jonah* mixed up with somebody else too. Wouldn't it be nice to just have ordinary birth parents? Confused high school kids, maybe, who realized that they weren't mature enough to raise a child themselves . . .

"Where did you go, that day at the library?" Katherine asked Angela. "Jonah saw you disappear."

"You mean, earlier this afternoon?" Angela asked.

"No, it was, like, three weeks ago," Katherine said.

Angela stared at her in disbelief.

"Get out!" she said. "Really?" She shook her head. "This time stuff can really mess with your mind. Honestly, to me it was just like an hour ago. Maybe an hour and a half."

Jonah squinted at her.

"Three weeks felt like an hour to you?" he said.

"Because I wasn't 'in time,' as JB calls it," Angela said. "He took me into this place called Outer Time, where we could spy on all of history. It's hard to describe, but it was kind of like being in an airplane and looking down on everything happening down on the ground. Or, I don't know, like Google Earth, where you can focus in close on one spot, then zoom out and get the broader view too."

"So JB and Hodge and Gary can zip back and forth through time?" Jonah said, with a sick feeling in the pit of his stomach. "They could go back and, I don't know, tackle me as I was walking into the cave a little bit ago, sending me back or forward in time that way? . . ."

The feeling of hopelessness was coming back. He pictured himself being sent back and forth endlessly, JB and Hodge fighting over him for centuries.

"No," Angela said. "It doesn't work that way. There's something else JB called the paradox of the doubles. No one can live through a particular time more than once. So, for example, there couldn't have been two or three copies of JB, jumped in from two or three different times, waiting at the back of the cave to attack Gary. Or two or three copies of me, either."

That made Jonah feel a little better.

"And," Angela continued, "I don't pretend to understand all of this, but because of your plane crashing into our time, where it didn't belong—where it changed lots of people's lives—because of that, we've all been living through what's known as Damaged Time. Kind of like a nuclear wasteland, maybe? When Mr. Hodge said that he couldn't get to you all for thirteen years, he really meant it. Time travelers couldn't get in at all for a long time. And they could see only limited moments in time—like some birthday party where you drank lots of Mountain Dew, Jonah?"

Jonah flushed with embarrassment. *I was only ten*, he wanted to protest. But Angela was still explaining.

"And then when they could get in," she said, "it was only at spots that they call points of damage—places where the pain of the time damage was most intense. Katherine, Jonah, you know how you saw JB at Mr. Reardon's office? How he appeared and disappeared?"

"Yeah," Jonah said. Katherine just nodded.

"That's because those were the only spots he could go to. Mr. Reardon was standing in the bathroom when he found out about the plane landing, and his boss was standing by that desk when he learned about the plane disappearing. So those were openings for JB," Angela said.

"But the other janitor came out into the waiting room," Jonah said. "The guy who gave me the Mountain Dew—"

"He truly was just a janitor for the FBI," Angela said. "JB bribed him to help."

At least that meant that the other janitor wasn't still hiding at the back of the cave, waiting to jump into the action.

Probably not anyway.

"So when JB gave us the file of names, what did he want us to do with it?" Jonah asked.

"He was just trying to temporarily increase the damage, so he could get closer to you," Angela said. "He didn't expect you to be enterprising enough to take pictures of the files and call the phone numbers and meet with me."

Katherine was grinning.

"I'm the one who thought of taking pictures," she whispered to Emily, even though Emily couldn't possibly have known what she was talking about.

"But all your enterprise just gave Gary an opening to try to grab you at the library," Angela added. "We had too many people in the same room at the same time with connections to the mysterious plane. And then you had those printouts of the witnesses and survivors lists. . . . I don't really understand how it works, but that created a huge doorway."

Katherine's grin faded a little.

Jonah was still trying to put it all together.

"So who sent the letters?" he asked. "JB or Hodge?"

"They each sent one," Angela said. "Again, so they could get in, get close to you. But they were racing each other, so they wrote the letters back in the 1990s, on ancient computers programmed for automatic printout— they routed their messages through the mail rooms of giant corporations, so your letters went through machines set up to automatically stuff envelopes with bills or credit-card offers."

"But the letters came in plain white envelopes," Jonah said.

"They programmed that," Angela said. "That worked

the way they wanted it to. But the old computers cut off parts of their messages. So they had to use other methods as well."

That was probably why they resorted to putting Post-it notes on the adoption papers, Jonah thought. And then when Jonah saw the mysterious figure searching his room, when Chip's computer files vanished—was that just to increase the "damage"? Each unexplained event had made Jonah and Chip and Katherine more paranoid and worried and scared. Had the other kids faced similar mysteries? Did it even matter who had done those things—JB or Hodge?

Angela was still talking.

"It took JB a long time to figure out that Hodge had chosen this adoption conference to steal you all back," she said. "JB thinks Hodge must have set up this cave twenty years ago, before the start of Damaged Time. He just had to trust that everything would stay ready. . . . Then Hodge and Gary broke hundreds of rules arranging for kids to move here, so they could pick up everyone at once. JB had to scramble to find all the addresses by looking at property records from the future."

Jonah felt dizzy, trying to figure out all the connections through time. *Future, past* . . . the words didn't have the same meanings he'd always counted on. In this strange new framework, the future could be the past, and the past could be the future, and . . .

"Oh, I see," Katherine said, as if *she* understood everything. "That's why it looked like the FBI knew Daniella McCarthy's new address before her parents had even made an offer on the house."

Angela nodded.

"Property transactions aren't always recorded accurately," she said. "Normally time travelers don't do things like that, relying on future addresses to send letters into the past. But this was a desperate case, because of Hodge and Gary. JB says they totally mucked up time."

Jonah could kind of picture it. He remembered a Boy Scout hike once where his troop had come upon a clear shallow stream. Jonah and a bunch of the other boys had jumped in and raced around splashing each other, even scooping up mud balls to throw at each other. The scoutmaster had given them a long lecture about disrupting nature—by the end of it, Jonah felt guilty about how many protozoans he'd probably killed. He could see how time could be like that clear stream. Probably Chip's family wasn't supposed to move; probably some other family was supposed to be in the house down the street from Jonah's house. And there had been at least twelve families who moved, at least twelve families whose lives were changed . . .

No, thirty-six families, Jonah thought, with a sudden

lump in his throat. *Mom and Dad weren't supposed to adopt me. Were they supposed to adopt some other kid? Was Katherine supposed to have a brother at all?*

Katherine seemed to be thinking along similar lines.

"So even if JB managed to fix all that time in the past— even if he sent all the kids back—how would he fix all the damage *now?*" she asked in a thick voice. "How would he tell my parents they don't have a son anymore?"

"I don't know," Angela admitted. "He's really worried about my nonexistent five kids too. The way he acts, you'd think one of them was going to be president some-day."

Jonah squinted off toward the other side of the room, thinking. Just then, he heard screams and saw kids jumping up in the group gathered around Gary.

No, not just kids—Gary himself.

"Hey!" Jonah screamed. "Who untied Gary?"

For that, improbably, was what seemed to have happened. With the ropes dragging uselessly behind him, Gary was racing across the room.

"Some kids are smart enough to know the future's the only choice!" Gary shouted.

"But—" Somehow Jonah had expected them all to vote on their decision. Didn't everyone believe in democracy?

Suddenly he realized where Gary was headed.

"Chip!" Jonah yelled. "Watch out!"

Gary was already slamming against Chip, jerking the Taser out of his hands before Chip had time to react. Gary whirled around, running again. He pointed the Taser at Jonah.

No—he was pointing it at Katherine.

"AHHHH!" Katherine screamed, crashing to the floor. The Elucidator dropped from her hand.

Jonah bent down to pick it up, but Gary was already there, pulling it away. And . . . punching in instructions, it seemed. He tucked the Taser under his arm and pounded in a whole string of coding on the Elucidator. Then he looked up, smirking, in JB's direction.

"Too bad, loser," Gary said mockingly. "I guess some of us are just better at being persuasive."

"No—you can't—" JB gasped.

"Do the age reversal first," Mr. Hodge suggested from across the room, completely ignoring JB. "This group will be easier to deal with as babies."

"Yes, sir," Gary said, grinning broadly as he punched more buttons. He took a step back and pointed the Elucidator toward Jonah and Katherine and all the other kids gathered around Angela.

"You feel well enough to stand up yet, sweetie?" he said to Katherine, who was still sprawled on the floor, recovering from the Taser blast. Emily was bent over her, quietly pulling the barbs out. "That would make things a little easier for me."

Katherine lifted her head.

"I'm not Daniella McCarthy!" she screamed. She had tears in her eyes—being Tasered must truly hurt. "I lied! I'm not one of your missing kids from history. I'm just— his sister!" She pointed at Jonah. "You have to let me go! You have to let everyone go!"

"No. That can't be." Mr. Hodge glared at Gary and hopped toward him, pulling against the ropes. "I thought you said the handprints all matched."

"They did," Gary insisted.

"I didn't touch the rock," Katherine said. "I just pretended. So you can't zap me."

Gary looked at Mr. Hodge, who'd stopped hopping. They both shrugged.

"Oh, well," Gary said. "Thirty-five treasures, one mistake." He smirked at Katherine. "I'm sure we'll find someone who might be willing to take you."

"You can't do this!" JB screamed. "That's another violation of time!"

Gary raised the Elucidator, pointing it carefully again.

"What will you tell our parents?" Katherine demanded.

"Freak rock cave-in. Such a tragedy," Gary said carelessly.

"Thirty-six children killed. And, sadly, the bodies will never be found."

Jonah thought about his parents losing both him and Katherine, all because Katherine had been so stubbornly loyal. It wasn't fair. It wasn't right. But what could he do? Gary had the Taser and the Elucidator. He had muscles in his arms thicker than Jonah's legs.

Jonah leaped at Gary anyway.

THIRTY-THREE

Even in midair, Jonah had no idea what he intended to *do* to Gary. Arm-wrestling him for the Elucidator or the Taser was out of the question. Punching him would be as useless as punching a brick wall.

So Jonah decided to take a page out of Katherine's book. With one hand, he grabbed for Gary's hair. With the other, he poked his fingers into Gary's eyes.

"Ow!" Gary screamed. Reflexively, he lifted his hands toward his face. The Taser clattered toward the ground.

Gary trapped it again with one foot.

Jonah let go of Gary's hair and grabbed for the Elucidator just as Gary was shoving him away, flinging him toward the stone wall.

Jonah slammed against the wall hard. He thought he could feel every bone of his spine hitting rock, one bone after the other. So it took him a few moments to realize . . .

The Elucidator was in his hand.

"Ha!" Jonah shouted at Gary.

Gary only smiled.

"It doesn't matter, kid," he said. "It's already programmed. That's one of the newer models—you don't even have to point it. We just do that out of habit."

Jonah looked down at the screen of the Elucidator, which seemed to be engaged in some kind of countdown: 10, 9, 8 . . .

As the 7 blinked onto the screen, Jonah threw the Elucidator as hard as he could, toward the far corner of the cave.

"JB!" he screamed. "Make it stop!"

Jonah could see JB catching the Elucidator, hitting buttons. Somehow Jonah managed to get up, to rush across the cave toward JB. Other kids had the same idea, flocking together toward JB. Jonah started to trip over something—the Taser? Wait a minute—where had Gary gone?

"Good-bye, friends," JB said softly. "I hope you enjoy time prison."

And then Mr. Hodge vanished, too, from right in the middle of the room.

Stunned, Jonah leaned over and scooped up the Taser. He kept running toward JB.

"Is it safe now?" Jonah asked. "Did you stop the countdown?"

JB still had his head bent over the Elucidator. He was still punching buttons. Jonah crowded close, with Chip and Katherine and Alex pressed in tightly beside him.

JB raised his head.

"I'm truly sorry," he said. "This is what I have to do."

He pointed the Elucidator at Alex, and Alex disappeared. Then he turned the Elucidator toward Chip.

"No!" Chip screamed.

Katherine clutched Chip's right arm and joined her screams to his. Jonah still had the Taser in his right hand, but there wasn't time to use that. He looped his right elbow around Chip's arm, hoping to hold him in place. With his left hand, Jonah made a swipe for the Elucidator.

The cave was already melting away.

"Noooooooo. . . ."

Jonah wasn't even sure who was screaming. Katherine? Chip? Himself? The Elucidator?

Hold on—the Elucidator?

He could feel it in his left hand. He was clutching it as tightly as he was clutching the Taser, as tightly as he had his arm wrapped around Chip's. But he couldn't see anything, because he had his eyes squeezed shut.

He dared to open one eye, just a crack.

He and Chip and Katherine seemed to be tumbling through the outer nothingness, but tumbling toward a vague hint of light, far off in the distance.

"Nooo. . . ."

This time he was sure: the wail was coming from the Elucidator, speaking in JB's voice.

"Jonah, there's been a mistake," JB's voice came out loud and clear and anxious, straight from the Elucidator. "You and Katherine have no business going into the fifteenth century with Chip and Alex. You're not allowed. You could cause even more damage. And you can't take the Elucidator or the Taser there—"

"You should have thought of that before you zapped Chip," Jonah said, and he was amazed that he could sound so defiant, out here in the middle of nothingness. "You should have known that we'd stick together."

There was a silence, as if JB was trying to accept that. Maybe he hadn't known they would stick together.

"Look, I'll tell you what to do so you and Katherine can come back," JB said, his voice strained.

"No," Jonah said stubbornly. "Tell us what to do so we can *all* come back. Even Alex."

Chip looked over at Jonah, gratitude gleaming in his eyes.

"Jonah," JB protested. "You don't know what you're talking about. Certain things have been set in motion. Chip and Alex *have* to go to the fifteenth century."

"Then Katherine and I are going too," Jonah said. He didn't know how it was possible, but he could feel time flowing past him, scrolling backward. He felt like he had only a few more seconds left to convince JB. "What if . . . what if we could fix the fifteenth century? Make everything right again? Then couldn't Alex and Chip come back to the twenty-first century with us?"

Silence.

Jonah had nervous tremors in his stomach. The hand holding the Elucidator was shaking. He wasn't even sure what he was asking for. But he couldn't stop now.

"You have to let us try," Jonah argued. "Let us try to save Alex and Chip *and* time. Or else . . ." He had to come up with a good threat. Or else what? Oh. "Or else we'll do our best to mess up time even worse than Hodge and Gary did."

The silence from the Elucidator continued. Jonah worried that they'd floated out of range, or that the battery had stopped working, just like a defective cell phone.

Then JB's voice came through again, faint but distinct.

"All right," he said wearily. "I'll let you try."

The lights on the horizon were getting brighter. Jonah knew nothing about the fifteenth century. He truly didn't know what he'd just bargained for.

"Wow," Chip said. "When you make a promise, you really keep it."

Promise? Jonah wondered. *What promise?* Then he remembered what he'd told Chip, right after Chip found out that he was adopted. *I swear, I'll do everything I can to help you.* It seemed like he'd said that hundreds of years ago, hundreds of lifetimes ago.

No—hundreds of years and lifetimes *ahead*.

Jonah's stomach gurgled. He could tell he was out of the nontime limbo because he was hungry again. Starving, in fact.

"Do you think they have good turkey legs in the fifteenth century?" he asked.

There was no time for Chip and Katherine to answer him or even to make fun of his question. The lights were getting brighter and brighter, rushing at them faster and faster and faster. . . .

They landed.

"Welcome to the fifteenth century," JB said grimly through the Elucidator. "Good luck."